Her moan was loud in the quiet of the room

Trish couldn't help herself. She was feeling totally free, wanton for the first time. And with Ty of all people—gorgeous, smart, sensitive, built. Totally built.

She let out a shuddering breath. His hands paused at her bare waist and their eyes locked. The moment was intoxicating. Like a drug, she didn't want it to end and thought she'd never get enough.

"I don't think this is smart," Trish managed.

His eyes were very green up close. His rough hands started to move again, stroking, touching one breast, then the other. "We're long past smart."

"I shouldn't be doing this." Her words were barely audible.

"You want it anyway," he whispered back.

And his mouth claimed hers in a deep, deep kiss.

Blaze™

Dear Reader,

Welcome to book two of SEX & THE SUPPER CLUB. To tell Trish's story, I interviewed screenwriters and producers to find out what life in the movie industry is really like. I never dreamed that the filmmaking process would strike so close to home. I would never have guessed that while I was in the middle of spinning the tale of Trish's screenwriting success, I'd find out that one of my own books had been made into a film by the Oxygen Network. *My Sexiest Mistake,* my debut book for the Harlequin Blaze line, was only the first. Word is, more of your favorite Blaze novels will follow, so keep your eyes peeled.

Meanwhile, I hope you enjoy Trish's story. Trish leads a quiet life—at least until her book starts—but what happens to her proves that there's a little bit of Blaze out there in all of us. Write me at kristin@kristinhardy.com and tell me what you think. Or visit my Web site at www.kristinhardy.com for contests, recipes and updates on my recent and upcoming releases, including the next SEX & THE SUPPER CLUB story, *Nothing but the Best,* coming in December 2004.

Have fun,

Kristin Hardy

Books by Kristin Hardy

HARLEQUIN BLAZE
44—MY SEXIEST MISTAKE
78—SCORING*
86—AS BAD AS CAN BE*
94—SLIPPERY WHEN WET*
148—TURN ME ON**

*Under the Covers
**Sex & the Supper Club

CUTTING LOOSE

Kristin Hardy

TORONTO • NEW YORK • LONDON
AMSTERDAM • PARIS • SYDNEY • HAMBURG
STOCKHOLM • ATHENS • TOKYO • MILAN • MADRID
PRAGUE • WARSAW • BUDAPEST • AUCKLAND

To the members of the
Wednesday Night Dinner Club
who gave me the idea,
and to Stephen,
who kept me inspired.

ISBN 0-373-79160-7

CUTTING LOOSE

Copyright © 2004 by Kristin Lewotsky.

All rights reserved. Except for use in any review, the reproduction or
utilization of this work in whole or in part in any form by any electronic,
mechanical or other means, now known or hereafter invented, including
xerography, photocopying and recording, or in any information storage
or retrieval system, is forbidden without the written permission of the
publisher, Harlequin Enterprises Limited, 225 Duncan Mill Road,
Don Mills, Ontario, Canada M3B 3K9.

All characters in this book have no existence outside the imagination of
the author and have no relation whatsoever to anyone bearing the same
name or names. They are not even distantly inspired by any individual
known or unknown to the author, and all incidents are pure invention.

This edition published by arrangement with Harlequin Books S.A.

® and TM are trademarks of the publisher. Trademarks indicated with
® are registered in the United States Patent and Trademark Office, the
Canadian Trade Marks Office and in other countries.

www.eHarlequin.com

Printed in U.S.A.

Prologue

Los Angeles, 1995

"COME ON, everyone, sit down, please." Trish Dawson glanced around the room at the managers for the university's spring play. Why the producer had asked Trish to run the meeting in her absence, Trish had no idea. Maybe she had a head for details, but she was much happier acting as script doctor than ringmaster. Thanks very much.

Trish took a deep breath. "Anita's sick so she's asked me to get things going. Now, we've got two weeks until opening night. We just need to do a status check before we start rehearsal. Martin, you first," she ordered, trying to avoid looking at the director with his razor-sharp cheekbones and spill of dark hair. He was too good-looking to trust, in Trish's book. She might have learned that lesson about men the hard way, but she'd learned it well.

"We're in pretty good shape," Martin allowed, flashing his careless smile. "Right now we're still running about ten minutes long. Where are you at on the cuts, Trish?"

"You'll have the revisions by noon tomorrow," she answered, mentally cursing the flush she could feel moving over her face.

"In that case, I'd like to plan for a dress rehearsal in a week," Martin said. "How are we doing with the battle scene?" he asked the dark-haired choreographer, Thea Masterson.

"Same as we were when you asked me an hour ago." Humor glinted in Thea's hazel eyes. "I've been running the cast through the sequences and they're coming along nicely."

"How about costumes?" Trish turned to her best friend, Cilla Danforth, wardrobe mistress. "Are we on target for dress rehearsal?"

"The outfits for the leads should be done," Cilla said, rolling up the cuff of her Marc Jacobs couture grunge shirt. "A couple of the bit players might have to play it in street clothes, but their costumes aren't that important."

"Historically accurate?" Martin asked.

Cilla stared at him blandly. "You worry about the actors, Martin, sugar. I'll worry about the clothes."

Cilla never took anything from anybody, Trish thought admiringly, wishing she could be the same way. "How about sets?" she asked, turning to the design manager, Paige Wheeler.

Paige consulted her tidy stack of notes. "Everything's ready," she supplied. "Touch-ups on the interior set for act three should be finished by tomorrow. Otherwise, everything's done."

The day Paige missed a deadline was the day the planets stopped moving in their orbits, Trish reflected. She looked at a blonde in a Pearl Jam T-shirt. "Delaney, where are we at on marketing?"

"Signage is up and Kelly's been running her 'Behind the Scenes' series in the school paper," Delaney responded, nodding toward Kelly Vandervere, staff reporter.

"And there's Sabrina," Kelly reminded her.

"Oh, right, thanks." Delaney turned to the group. "You guys all probably know Sabrina Pantolini, the one who's doing the documentary on the play. She's going to cut a commercial from her footage to play on the college station."

There was a round of applause. Trish waited for it to die down and checked her watch. "Great, so it looks like everything's on schedule. I'll just write this up for Anita and we can get started with rehearsals."

Everyone rose and began drifting out. "S&S meeting tonight at Tortilla Flats," Cilla reminded her before leaving.

"S&S? What's that?" asked Martin, standing nearby.

Tell him it stood for Sex & Supper Club? No way was Trish going to go there, especially not when her palms were already sweating from nerves. "Just a group of us getting together," she said vaguely, picking up her notebook.

He considered. "Maybe I'll come along."

To hear them dissect which guy they knew kissed better than the rest? Trish resisted snorting. "It's, um, a girl-only thing."

"Maybe some other time, then," he said lightly. "So, are you nervous about opening night?"

"A little," she admitted. "Are you?"

"Not really. It'll be fine."

"I wish I had your faith."

He shrugged. "It's not hard. It's just a matter of trusting to luck."

She met his eyes for the first time. "I guess everything is."

1

Los Angeles, Present

"SO THIS is your favorite sex fantasy, jeans and a T-shirt? All this time, I never knew you were acting out your dreams at the Supper Club meetings." Cilla looked out the door of her '30s Brentwood bungalow, an impish look on her triangular vixen's face as she stared at Trish and her casual clothes.

"You guys always turn me on so much," Trish said, walking through the door.

"I'll bet. You do realize you're going to have to change, right? Remember? 'Dress like your favorite sex fantasy?'"

"'To see my fantasy become reality.' Yep, I read the invitation, too."

"Sabrina's serious about her costume parties."

"Right. Well, just now my favorite sex fantasy involves a bath and a foot massage," Trish sighed, setting her purse down on the hall table. Working for her sister Amber, at her home concierge company, doing errands for a living, was exhausting. "I am beat. Anyway, you're one to talk." She gestured at Cilla's plum-colored Michael Kors business suit. "Where's your costume?"

"I just got home. The big Danforth's couture show is tomorrow, so of course everything went wrong all day long."

"Rodeo Drive retail. It's a rough life you live," she said with false sympathy as Cilla stuck out her tongue. "So is it all taken care of now?"

"I think so. We've got someone to pick up the designer when she flies in, so I'm off the hook for the night. And I do have a costume for the party, I'll have you know. I'm going as a naughty nurse," Cilla said, flipping back the neckline of her blouse to flash her the black lace of her bra.

Trish fanned herself laughingly. "You keep that up, you'll give your patients heart failure."

"Oh, but what a nice way for them to go," Cilla grinned. "So I'm set, but we've got to do something about you." Suddenly her eyes brightened in a way Trish didn't entirely trust. "You know, it's only seven-thirty," she said casually. "We've got buckets of time. Let's get a drink and we can fix you right up."

Trish flopped down in one of the overstuffed chairs as Cilla walked to the kitchen. "It's been a long day. I'm as fixed up as I need to be."

Cilla popped her head out of the kitchen doorway. "If you go like this, you'll feel totally uncomfortable and be convincing yourself to leave half an hour after you get there." She ducked back into the kitchen.

Trish raised her voice. "I'll be ready to leave after half an hour anyway. You know how much I love parties. Right up there next to root canals."

"So don't think of it as a party. Think of it as a Sex

& Supper Club meeting with a few extra people there. Come on. Just this once, trust me." Cilla walked out, carrying fizzing glasses of something pale. "I'll make you look so gorgeous you'll be the toast of the evening. Now what happened with the hunky carpenter you were talking to when I called you this afternoon?"

Trish shrugged. "He finished the job and left. They usually do."

"That's all? You didn't talk with him?"

"Of course I talked with him. I had to get him to sign the paperwork, didn't I?"

Cilla blinked. "You spend half a day in a house alone with a gorgeous man and you don't even flirt with him? Trish, Trish, Trish, what are we going to do with you?" She clicked her tongue in disappointment.

"The client could have walked in. Besides, he's a contractor we use regularly. If I'd joked back with him, he might have gone ahead and asked me out." Trish said, and took a sip of her drink. Ginger ale.

"So? He might have been a nice guy."

Trish swirled her drink around. "Yeah, but if we went out, I'd have to talk with him, and then I'd be all stressed over saying something clever so of course I wouldn't be able to think of a single thing, and then I'd be worried about the silence and then I'd be worried that he would be thinking I was a boring goob and wondering how to end the evening as soon as possible. And there's the whole kissing thing at the end of the night, and I'm starting to think I'm just not cut out for it." She took a drink. "And if we hit it off, it would be worse. I'd spend way too much money on haircuts and new underwear and then he'd break up with me and I'd have to work with him later. It's just not worth all the hassle." Trish looked up at Cilla, who was suppressing a smile. "What?"

"That's efficient. You got all the way through the entire relationship without even leaving the room, let alone talking to the guy. Look at all the money and time you saved."

Trish flushed. "Look, it's just more than I want to mess with right now."

"It doesn't have to be that hard," Cilla pointed out. "He might have been a really funny guy and all you'd have had to do was sit there and laugh." She leaned in toward Trish. "Who knows, you might even have had fun. Look, do me a favor."

"What?" Trish gave her a suspicious look.

"Forget about all that stuff. Come to the party and just relax. The gang will be there so you don't have to worry about talking to guys all alone. Besides, I'll get you fixed up so they'll talk to you no matter what. Consider it an experiment." She rose, slender and leggy in her short skirt. "You might even have a good time."

Trish eyed Cilla skeptically and followed her as she headed down the hall. "You're not going to turn into my sister and start telling me it's all about appearance, are you?"

"That's just Amber's excuse for making you do all the grunt work while she stays in the office filing her nails."

"It's her company," Trish said simply. "Besides, she's better at the sales end. Amber likes dressing up every day, I'm happy in jeans. Someone's got to show the right image to the outside world."

"Gee, can't imagine who said that." Cilla's voice was wry. "You know, if you just ditched the T-shirt and jeans and spruced yourself up a little, people would be so busy staring at you, no one would give Amber a second glance."

Trish flicked her gaze to the ceiling. "I don't want people staring at me, thanks, and I like wearing a T-shirt and jeans."

"And they like you," Cilla said smoothly. "But at a party? You'll feel more comfortable if you're looking your best."

"Come on, Cilla, a little makeup isn't going to change things."

"Mmm. I had in mind something a little more radical," Cilla stated, walking into her bedroom and pulling open the closet door.

"If you think I'm going to be able to fit into anything of yours, you're dreaming," Trish said, coming in after her. "I'm three sizes larger than you are."

"Give me a break." Cilla grabbed a handful of the cloth at Trish's waist. "You could take these jeans off without ever unbuttoning them. Why are you still buying clothes for someone you were ten years ago?"

"They're comfortable," Trish muttered.

"So's being naked, but I don't see you walking around like that."

"This is ridiculous."

Cilla pulled out garments at random, humming to herself. "Humor me."

Trish tried again. "Cilla, no one's going to care whether I'm in costume or not.

Cilla turned to her and smiled. "Trust me. They will when I get through with you."

"LET ME SEE."

"Stay still."

"I just want to make sure you're not going overboard."

"I'm not."

"I don't believe you," Trish said, trying unsuccessfully to rise from her perch on the toilet seat.

"You'll see when I'm done. Now sit," Cilla ordered, pushing her back down. She brandished the mascara wand. "Look toward the ceiling and try to keep your eyes open wide."

"That's the third coat of mascara you've put on," Trish pointed out. Makeovers exasperated her. Good, bad or ugly, she was who she was, and all shining-up her act was going to do was make her expect things that were never going to happen.

Yeah, she'd learned that the hard way.

Trish reached out for the hand mirror on the counter but Cilla fixed her with a look. "You take one peek and I'm not giving your jeans back. Ever."

"Come on, Cilla, I'm feeling like your personal Frankenstein monster, here. I can put on my own lipstick."

"Uh-uh." Cilla came back from her makeup drawer with a lipstick the color of ripe cherries. "I want you to get the full impact."

The full impact was what Trish was worried about as she worked to keep her mouth still under the tickle of Cilla's lipstick brush. Simple, low-key and in the background, that was the way she liked it.

Cilla finished and set the lip color down, then she stepped back with her hands on her hips and studied her friend. "Now that's a sight to see," she said in satisfaction, and then laughed. "That was the most scared I've seen you look since that time we ordered a male stripper for your birthday."

"Just tell me I don't look like Tammy Faye."

"You don't look like Tammy Faye," Cilla assured her. "Okay, upsy daisy, but don't look at the mirror in here." She covered Trish's eyes until they got into the bedroom. "I want you to get the total effect all at once."

"I'll get the total effect if I trip and break my neck."

"Almost there, almost there…okay, you're in front of the mirror. Are you ready?"

Despite herself, Trish felt a little tingle of anticipation. "So show me."

"Ta-da," Cilla sang and dropped her hands.

For a moment, all Trish could do was stare. And a gorgeous stranger in the mirror stared back at her. The other "her" stood with a silky waterfall of absolutely smooth red-gold hair flowing to her waist and a mouth as tempting as chocolate. The features that had always seemed too delicate in comparison to her sister's sun-tossed California blond looks were suddenly vivid and underscored with some special importance. Expert makeup played up the hollows in her cheeks and rendered her slate-gray eyes dark and somehow mysterious. "Wow." She raised her hands to the soft strands of her hair. "Wow," she said again.

"Do you like it?"

"I'm…wow, Cilla, really. I'm amazed." With a little surge of excitement, Trish turned to and fro to get the full effect. And, she had to admit, in the outfit she wore, it was some effect indeed. The evening required a bold statement, Cilla had decreed. Digging in her closet, she'd come up with her best studded-leather dominatrix look. To Trish's amazement, she'd actually been able to zip it up, although taking a deep breath made her breasts swell upward alarmingly. The leather bustier molded her waist, the skirt fit her like a second skin. Fishnet tights and high-heeled red ankle boots completed the ensemble. It might have been couture, but it looked like something out of an S&M club.

And it looked really fabulous.

Still, she wasn't sure she was such a good judge of party wear. "Are you sure this isn't a little over the top?"

"Are you kidding? At a do like this?" Cilla sniffed. "You'll be tame. Too bad we couldn't get you a whip," she added thoughtfully. "It would add that little extra touch."

"For that 'you've been a bad boy lately' look?"

"Like I said, you never know. You might enjoy it."

Trish rolled her eyes. "Hardly. Although it feels like the person I'm dressed up as would." She turned to inspect herself from behind.

"That's the fun part, isn't it?" Cilla said cheerfully,

slipping into her nurse's costume. "Haven't you ever wanted to do that, be someone else just for a night?"

Trish's standard answer was that who she was would have to do. If she wasn't one-hundred-percent thrilled with life, that was only to be expected. She'd shed the crazy expectations of being a siren, of having men tumble at her feet, of finding true love with Mr. Right. She just wasn't built for it. Her friends could tell her she was a hopeless romantic all they liked. Wanting love and believing that it had any place in her life were two very different things.

For one night, though, maybe it could be different. Maybe for this night she could be someone else, see how the other half lived.

Slowly the corners of her mouth curved up into a smile and she vamped in the mirror. "Be someone else, li'l ol' me?"

"Why not?" Cilla slicked her dark-gold hair back behind her ears and hung a stethoscope around her neck. "In this getup, you could have yourself a time. What do you think?"

Trish grinned at her reflection. "I think we'd better get to the party."

FORTY MINUTES LATER, as they stood outside Sabrina's house, the notion seemed altogether less brilliant. Sabrina lived in Venice, a small neighborhood south of Santa Monica. An ambitious developer in the thirties had built a neighborhood of houses along a series of narrow, criss-crossing canals dug into the California soil. Now, newly dredged and fashionable, the neighborhood held echoes of the real Venice or Amsterdam, with its small arched bridges and houses next to the water.

It definitely didn't go with dominatrix-wear. "I can't believe I thought this was a good idea," Trish murmured, pulling futilely at her skirt as they made their way up the walkway to Sabrina's house. It was one thing to be wearing the outfit in Cilla's bedroom; it was another to wear it in public. Not even the silk duster she'd thrown over the top helped.

"Stop picking at your clothes," Cilla scolded.

"It's too tight."

"It's Gaultier. It's supposed to fit like that."

"How come I've never seen you in it, then?"

Cilla shrugged and twirled her stethoscope playfully. "You know couture. You can get away with wearing it once, but that's about it."

"So this is my one big chance?"

"Make the most of it," Cilla advised, then groped in her candy-colored Louis Vuitton Murakami bag as her cell phone burbled for attention. "Hello?"

Trish walked a few steps away, adjusting her bustier. Okay, so maybe she felt like the lead actress in some 1960s French sex farce. She just needed to get into character. It wouldn't be her walking into the party, it would be her alter ego, the one who loved being outrageous and living at the center of the whirlwind. It would be okay.

"You have got to be kidding," Cilla burst out from behind her. "What happened to the escort? On second thought, I don't care. Send her a limo. I've got a party to go to." Cilla paced a few steps, tension vibrating in every line of her body. "All right, all right, fine," she said shortly. "I'm in Venice. I'll be there in twenty minutes." She ended the call and cursed viciously.

Trish stared. "What was that about?"

Cilla turned to face her. "Apparently our designer for the couture show tomorrow isn't satisfied with our events coordinator picking her up at the airport and taking her to dinner. She's insisting that I do it."

"Why you?"

Cilla blew out a breath of frustration. "We've met once or twice at her shows."

"Not to mention the fact that your family owns Danforth's and the entire Forth's chain and has more money than God."

"Please." Cilla rolled her eyes. "The show coordinator says she's threatening to walk. I don't really have a choice."

"What do you mean?"

"I've got to go get her."

"But…but what about the party?" Trish asked with a spurt of panic. "I thought we were going together."

"I have to do it," Cilla said apologetically. "It's only for a little while. If necessary I'll haul her back here—there is no way I'm missing Sabrina's documentary."

"Maybe I can go with you," Trish tried, despising the tone in her voice.

Cilla shook her head and buttoned up her coat to hide most of her costume. "I can only imagine the fit she'd have if you show up in Gaultier. Prima donna doesn't begin to cover it. Besides, someone has to tell Sabrina.

Hey, you look fabulous." She gave Trish a quick hug. "Go in and find the rest of the gang. You'll be fine."

Trish watched Cilla hurry off to her car and she glanced down the alley to the canal bridge glimmering at the end. If she could only snap her fingers and be back in her nice, quiet apartment for the night. She'd light some candles, pour a glass of wine, and maybe watch a movie or work on the screenplay she was writing.

Instead, shyness was going to smother her in rooms full of strangers, while she tried to look as though she had something more to do than go to the bathroom again and again because it was a place to hide for a few minutes. Home, even if she had to walk, sounded infinitely more appealing.

But Sabrina was expecting her. More to the point, Sabrina was expecting *them,* and Trish really ought to go explain.

And one way or another, she had to find a ride home or at least get a taxi.

All the good reasons in the world didn't mask the fact that walking through Sabrina's door was about the least appetizing prospect she could imagine. If she'd been in her normal clothes, it would have been bad enough, but going inside all alone, wearing the most revealing outfit she'd ever worn in her life? Looking at it from above, the bustier was outrageously low-cut. Her breasts billowed up out of it like newly risen bread. Cilla couldn't expect her to do this, Trish thought desperately. What if she were the only person in costume? What if she looked as ridiculous as she felt? The mem-

ory of the Trish she'd seen in Cilla's mirror receded to
a pinpoint and the Trish in the now just stood on the
porch and swallowed, feeling miserably conspicuous.

Sabrina, she reminded herself. This was Sabrina's
special night and she wanted her friends there to celebrate with her. It wasn't about Trish, it was about Sabrina.

It was about being a good friend.

"Oh, don't be such a wuss," Trish muttered to herself. No one was going to care what she looked like.
They'd probably all be too busy worrying about themselves. Besides, odds were she'd never even see most
of these people again. "Just do it," she told herself
fiercely.

And rang the bell.

When the door opened, though, it wasn't Sabrina
there. It was a sandy-haired boy who looked no more
than sixteen or seventeen, the top of his head approxi-
mately at her eye level.

She couldn't possibly in her panic have walked up
to the wrong door, Trish thought wildly. Please, God,
let her be at the right house.

"Wow," he said appreciatively. "I guess you're here
for the party. My name's Lee. Wanna run away and
elope?"

Despite herself, she laughed. He looked barely old
enough to drive, let alone put the moves on her. "Give
me a minute or two to get the prenup in order."

"Fair enough. Come on in and we can discuss it." He
stepped back and swung the door wide.

Sabrina's living room surged with activity. A woman

in neck-to-ankle red latex was tangoing with a man wearing a dog collar. A Wild-West saloon girl leaned over a shirtless construction worker sprawled on a couch. There were hookers, police officers, Catholic schoolgirls, sheiks, a pizza-delivery boy, and even what Trish assumed was a Marquis de Sade in a pale-blue frock coat and wig.

"Let me take your coat," Lee said, whisking it off her before she could protest.

And then she stood in front of the room in just her outfit.

One head after another turned to look at Trish. She stifled the urge to flee. Maybe a seam had split, she speculated, feeling her face heat. Maybe one of her breasts had popped out entirely. It would be just her luck. Or maybe her outfit was just too much, period. Granted, most people were in costume, but she hadn't really seen anyone in quite as outrageous a getup as hers. Then, across the room, she saw a sleek, exotic-looking woman dressed in eye-popping leather.

With a start, Trish realized it was her reflection, thrown back at her from an ornate mirror hanging on the wall.

Giddiness rushed through her. Sabrina's guests weren't staring because she looked ridiculous, they were staring because she looked good. Gaping wouldn't do, and yet Trish wanted nothing more than to rush over to the looking glass and drink it all in, gawk at her image until she could convince herself that it was really her. For tonight, anyway.

But oh, what a night it would be.

Sabrina's home was built vertically, the rooms rising around a central atrium, each side offset half a story from the other so that the rooms stairstepped up from one another. Trish glanced up and found her gaze snagged by that of the Marquis de Sade, who leaned carelessly on the waist-high barrier of the open loft overlooking the living room. Thin leather strips dangled from the ebony handle of his flail. An ornate silver mask covered his face from the hairline of his white-powdered wig to below his nose. Trish could see only his mouth, defined by the clean lines of a modified Vandyke. And she could see his eyes, looking out through the holes in the mask.

Staring directly at her.

Trish glanced to either side to see if he was looking at someone else, and then back up to find his gaze still pinned to hers. Something skittered through her veins. The thing was not to get embarrassed. She looked good, she knew it. Better than good. Maybe that was why he was staring, or maybe he was admiring her outfit. Maybe he was into Gaultier. Perhaps, she thought with a smile, he thought he was looking at a kindred spirit.

Lee the doorman nudged her. "So, can I get you a drink?"

"What?" Trish blinked, dragging her gaze away from the Marquis. "Um, actually I should probably find Sabrina first."

"My cousin? I saw her a couple minutes ago. I'll show you."

"Are you even old enough to be at a party like this?" Trish asked, squinting at him.

"Are you kidding?" He gave her an affronted look. "I'm at UCLA. I'm almost nineteen."

It wouldn't do to smile. "Oops, my mistake."

"I can think of one or two ways you can make it up to me."

She gave a startled laugh. "Sorry, cradle-robbing is not my thing."

"Once you try it, baby, you'll never go back." He gave her what was probably meant to be a roguish wink, although he had to narrow both eyes a bit to do it.

"I'll let you know if I change my mind," Trish promised, struggling to keep a straight face. She tensed, though, when he started toward the staircase that zigzagged its way up the side of the atrium. Toward the Marquis. "Where are you going?"

Lee glanced back at her. "You wanted to go to Sabrina. She's up on the roof with some friends, I think."

The Marquis watched her walk across the room. And he wasn't the only one, she realized uncomfortably, catching a head or two turning out of the corner of her eye. She glanced again at her image in the mirror across the room. *That's who you are tonight,* she reminded herself and laughed. *Work it.* A cowboy with his shirt unbuttoned to his navel winked at her and hefted the lariat he held. "I've been really bad, mistress. Want to tie me up and teach me a lesson?"

Trish gave him a mock severe look. "It'll take more than just rope to teach you a proper lesson."

"I'll be waiting."

Lee led her up the risers of the stairs. She could feel the gaze of the Marquis on her. Being watched like that added an exaggerated level of self-awareness to her every move. She climbed the stairs, knowing he was studying her. She pushed back the spill of her hair, knowing he would see. Then the plaster bulk of the next flight of stairs crossed between them, blocking her view of the Marquis, at least until she nearly reached the landing.

Anticipation had her wondering what it would be like to see him up close. Then suddenly she was stepping onto the landing at the level of the loft, practically close enough to reach out and touch him. A current of air whispered over her bare shoulders and brought out goose bumps on her skin. She swore she saw his eyes darken. He stared at her, running his fingers slowly through the knotted thongs of his flail.

It suddenly seemed outrageously erotic.

Their gazes locked with the snapping jolt of static electricity. Her footsteps slowed. Something about the fact that the mask obscured most of his face focused her attention on the lean line of his jaw and the hint of a cleft in his chin. As though he knew what she was looking at, one corner of his mouth twitched into a smile. He brought two fingertips to his lips and blew her a mocking kiss.

Trish flushed and started up the next flight of stairs.

And finally she was at roof level and stepping out into the cool night air. A small knot of people stood at the far end, looking out at the lights of the city. A glance at them calmed the nerves that danced in her belly, because she knew these people almost as well as she knew herself.

The laughing woman with the cap of dark hair was Sabrina, and at her side her lover, Stef. Irrepressible Kelly waved her hand around as she told a story with the help of her boyfriend Kev, who, as usual, looked as if he'd been hacking at his hair with garden shears. Delaney, still the corn silk blonde, hooted. Maybe the generic-looking man at her side was her date, Trish speculated. Or maybe not. More likely he was there with cool, self-possessed Paige. He had that innocuous, trust-fund-preppie look that most of her men seemed to have.

They might all be older and wiser, but the Sex & Supper Club was still together, and just as close as they'd ever been. She would have walked through fire for any one of them.

After all, she'd walked into the party alone, hadn't she?

Sabrina swung toward them in the dimness. "Hey, Elliot, who's your friend?" she asked casually.

Trish gave Lee a sidelong glance. "Elliot?"

He blushed. "My friends call me Lee."

"Oh my God, it's Trish!" Kelly yelped, suddenly breaking away from the group and rushing over to Trish. "I didn't recognize you. You look amazing."

In an instant, Trish was surrounded. "Look at your hair," Delaney said, running her fingers through the silky strands. "You look like something out of a *Vogue* spread."

Trish couldn't stop the grin. "Cilla did it. You know her, just some old rag from her closet."

"Yeah, an old rag that cost about as much as a small

car. So who knew you were a size three?" Kelly marveled.

"Size five, Cilla says," Trish corrected in embarrassment.

"Like that's any more real than a three," Kelly said unconcernedly. "Where is Cilla, anyway?"

"She had to go take care of something for her fashion show tomorrow. She said she'll be here in a couple of hours. Where's Thea?"

"She's got the flu, poor baby," Sabrina contributed. "Called me sounding like a seal. Not feeling her friskiest." She gave Trish a mischievous look. "So, the real Trish at last?"

Trish grinned. "It's not the real Trish, it's my alter ego."

Kelly snorted. "Are you kidding? You could look this good all the time."

"Oh, yeah. I can just imagine how thrilled my sister would be if I showed up at the office for my list of errands and things wearing leather and studs."

"Seriously, though," Kelly persisted. "Forget the leather. With very little effort you could look amazing enough to have men eating out of your hands."

She wasn't at all sure that she wanted to be that conspicuous. "I think you're exaggerating."

"Oh, yeah?" Sabrina countered. "Let's ask Elliot."

"Lee," Trish corrected her in an undertone.

Sabrina raised her eyebrows. "Lee?"

"Cut him some slack," Trish murmured, "he's trying to grow up. Everybody should be allowed to change."

A smile stole over Sabrina's face. "You're right," she said, and swung around to look at her cousin, who was talking with Stef and Kev. "Hey, Lee," she called, "what do you think of Trish, here?"

He glanced over. "Hey, I wanted to get married. She was the one who shot me down."

Sabrina turned back to the group. "There, see?"

Trish rolled her eyes. "He's just a kid, Sabrina."

"Well, we'll just have to take a bigger poll. The casting director for *Runway Dreams* is here somewhere."

Kelly raised an eyebrow. "Rob Carroll? You do run with a hot crowd."

"He's *the* Mr. L.A. right now," Sabrina said.

"And sleeps with anything that moves," quipped Kelly.

"Picky, picky. We'll find another man. Shoot, my famous cousin said he'd stop by later."

"You mean me?" Lee called over.

"No, my other superstar cousin," Sabrina said fondly.

"You mean Ty Ramsay, box-office hero?" Kelly asked. "Wait a minute. I thought you swore you'd never let him near anyone you cared about."

Sabrina gave a bashful look. "I shouldn't have said that. I was just ticked because he'd played hit-and-run with a girlfriend of mine."

"Your friends ought to know better. You've warned us often enough," Paige pointed out.

"He's actually a pretty cool guy as long as you're not dating him," Sabrina said. "His problem is that he's just a terminal romantic with ADD."

"You know, I saw him interviewed one time about Megan Barnes back when they were engaged," Delaney said. "The way he talked about her was really sweet. He seemed totally sincere."

"He *is* totally sincere," Sabrina said, "fatally so, at least at the time. It's just a month or so later when the buzz wears off and he comes back down to earth that's the problem."

"Okay, well, who else have you got?" Kelly demanded.

"There's Kyle Franklin. He's—"

"In the interest of the brotherhood, I've got to break this up," interrupted Kev, walking up behind Kelly to slide his hands around her waist. "Lay off the poor guys. We can't all have flawless taste and judgment." He kissed her ear and Kelly gave a goofy smile.

"But give us credit," Stef said, coming up beside Sabrina to tangle his fingers in hers. "We usually figure it out."

"That you do," Sabrina said, beaming at him.

"Don't you guys start doing that cute couple thing," Delaney warned, turning to include Paige and her date, as well, who weren't even remotely doing cute. "You're not going to win me over. Some of us are just fine and dandy being single. In fact, some of us like it." She linked arms with Trish and gave a naughty grin. "Now if you'll excuse us bachelorettes, we're going downstairs to play the field."

2

TRISH STOOD in Sabrina's loft, where the caterers had set up the sushi bar, idly sipping sake and staring out the glass wall into the night. Delaney had drifted off to dance. Normally, then, Trish would have started planning her exit but not this time. She'd never been to a party quite like this one. The hours floated by in a haze of laughter. Every time she stopped moving, she was drawn into conversation. Men smiled, flirted, and it didn't matter that she was too nervous to talk much because they did the talking for her.

And always, always when she looked up, the Marquis was watching her with that enigmatic smile. Somehow watching him watch her made her savor it all the more. Would he approach? she wondered. *Just a matter of time,* the words rose in her mind, and she laughed. Whenever she'd heard women say that, she'd wondered how they could be so absurdly confident, how it was that they didn't understand how capricious romance could be. Suddenly, though, half intoxicated with her own power, she understood.

Trish raised her sake cup to her lips and tasted only air. It was empty, she realized. Turning to the table that held the carafes of different sake, she studied the information cards and reached out.

"It's bad luck to pour your own sake."

She knew it was him before she saw the blue brocade at her elbow. Somehow she'd known he'd have a voice like that, deep, with just a faint whisper of roughness. It was the kind of voice that could mesmerize a woman, the kind of voice that put her on her guard. Taking her time, Trish moved to face him.

And saw the sea green of his eyes.

When she'd been in fifth grade, Trish had gotten hit in the stomach during a dodge-ball game. It had been like this, that sudden, helpless sense of all the air rushing from her lungs, that shocking, indisputable contact. From across the room, he'd intrigued; this close, he riveted. His eyes should have been cool, with their mix of blue and green and gray. Somehow, though, they shone with an intensity, a heat that left her staring helplessly back.

Then they crinkled in humor and released her.

Trish gave a shaky laugh and handed him her cup. "I'll pour yours if you pour mine," she said lightly.

"At your service, mistress," he said, with a bow. "And which would you like? We've got *bichu wajo*, if you like herb overtones," he read off the information card. "Or how about *koi no kawa*? That translates as 'love river,' by the way," he added, lifting the carafe temptingly.

"How could I say no to a name like that?" she asked, hit with a sudden, almost unrecognizable urge to flirt.

He poured a tasting into her cup. "I'll take that as a good sign."

It was strange being so close to him, Trish thought,

and yet somehow familiar, perhaps because they'd been watching each other since she'd arrived. The mask focused her attention on his mouth, which was taut enough to make her certain he was strong, enticing enough to make her wonder what it would feel like to kiss him.

And wonder what his face would look like uncovered.

She sipped the wine and nodded, holding out her cup for more. She watched as he filled her glass. Sandy-brown hair, maybe, or blond, she thought, judging by the Vandyke and the light hairs on the back of his wrist. He had the long fingers and corded tendons of some artisan skilled with his hands, and he passed her the sake with a careless grace.

Trish raised her eyes from her cup to his face. "And you, my lord? What would please you?"

"Choosing just one thing would be the trick," he said, rubbing his knuckles against his jaw. "And will you obey my command if I do?"

Butterflies tickled her stomach. "A dominatrix serving the Marquis? It's sort of like an irresistible force meeting an immovable object, isn't it?"

He considered. "Something of an impasse, it's true."

"I suppose we could arm wrestle."

"Hardly seems fair to you."

"Don't be too sure," she disagreed. "All that whipping keeps me in shape."

His smile widened. "So I see. Maybe I'll just settle for talking you into pouring me some sake and coming out on the deck."

She felt a little self-conscious as he watched her choose a cup and pour the wine, but there was pleasure in being the object of his attention. "Your drink, my lord," she said, inclining her head.

A corner of his mouth twitched as he took the cup she offered and clicked it against hers. "To unexpected pleasures."

Trish flushed. "Unexpected pleasures," she echoed.

Outside, the air was faintly cool with the first breath of fall. The dark water of the canal that ran along in front of Sabrina's house reflected the stars. The trees glimmered with fairy lights, the same winking dots that outlined the curved stone bridges that crossed the water. "It doesn't seem real. It's like a little slice of Italy, isn't it?" Trish leaned on the railing. "Only in L.A."

"Land of play-acting?" he asked, walking up to stand beside her.

"Indeed." He was taller than she was, Trish realized, even though she was wearing heels. She caught a whiff of something clean that might have been cologne, or perhaps just soap. Whatever it was, it smelled all male. Adrenaline sang in her veins. "And are you play-acting tonight, Marquis?"

"No more than you. You wear it well, by the way. It almost looks real."

She sipped her sake and gave him an amused look. "Maybe it is."

"I don't think so."

"Maybe I worked late and didn't have time to change."

"So you came straight over here exhausted from all

that whipping and getting your feet kissed?" Behind the mask, his eyes gleamed with humor. "Just lost track of time, did you?"

"You know how it is," Trish said flippantly. "When you love what you do, it doesn't seem like work."

He studied her, his head tilted to one side, then shook it briskly. "Nope, don't buy it. I don't see you getting off on spanking some balding, overweight CEO."

"Ah, but that's just it. You just don't know, do you?" She propped a hand on the wide, wooden railing and slid the other down the curve of her waist. "'Neath this quiet exterior could lie the soul of a committed disciplinarian," she said, riding the giddy rush of fun. Perhaps it was the anonymity of the mask that set her free. If she could see his whole face, he'd probably be the kind of good-looking guy who would make her freeze up. Dressed as he was, he was just a pair of hot eyes and a silky voice, a presence in the night. "Just wait until you're in my clutches and don't have a choice."

Immediately, he seemed much closer. "Oh? Am I going to be in your clutches tonight?"

Her breathing tightened. "I suppose that's up to you." A beat went by.

"Mmm. The Marquis de Sade as a submissive? No, there would be riots in S&M land."

Amusement bubbled up and quickly the tension evaporated. "You could tell them you're finding your feminine side."

The Marquis laughed. "I'd prefer your feminine side."

It felt different, Trish realized abruptly. She wasn't uncomfortable, she wasn't tongue-tied. She wasn't miserable and hoping she could leave. She was actually having fun.

And she was turned on.

"Does that mean you're asking me to take you on as a client, after all?"

"Brings us back to that irresistible force problem, doesn't it?"

"No dominatrix worth her salt would let a client wear a mask without her permission. Take it off so I can see your face, and then I'll decide."

"You want me to take it off?" He set down his sake cup and raised one hand toward his face.

Anticipation had her pulse thudding a little faster. "I like to know who I'm dealing with."

"That's less about the looks and more about the person, isn't it? Image shouldn't be everything, even in L.A."

"That's usually my line," she said ruefully.

He inclined his head. "Thanks for the loan."

"Still, it's hardly fair that you get to see my face and I don't get to see yours."

He chuckled softly. "Perhaps I have my reasons."

"You can always put it back on." The urge to see his face was fast becoming a craving.

He just drained his sake cup. "It's a slippery slope, mistress. Some things cannot be undone."

"Coward," she mocked him.

A corner of his mouth tugged up in amusement and he glanced down at the flail that stuck out of his pocket. "Careful what you call a man who's holding a whip."

Trish laughed. "Good point. In that case, can I get you some more sake, my lord?"

"Only if you promise to continue our conversation when you return."

"It might be bad for my reputation if I follow your orders." She didn't want to leave. She wanted to stay and bask in this new feeling.

"Look at it as coincidence. What I want just happens to be what you feel like doing." He reached out for her hand and brought it to his lips.

It was the contrast that did it. Cool air, warm lips. Rough wood, soft skin. The touch of another where there hadn't been one in so long. For an instant, it was as though every nerve in her body were centered in the small patch of skin over her knuckles and she could only absorb it. She thought *more*, and *I want* and *don't stop*.

He lowered her hand and closed her fingers around the ceramic sake cup.

Her alter ego no doubt would have had something sexy and provocative to say. Trish considered it a triumph that she remained upright and mobile.

The Marquis gave her a mischievous look. "Sake?" he asked.

She walked back inside, closing the sliding door behind her.

It was two different worlds, the quiet, private dimness of the deck outside and the warmth and hubbub of indoors. Trish turned to the sake bar, looking out into the night to see the Marquis watching her. She was trembling a bit, and yet talking with him, being with him didn't tie her in knots the way it did with other men. It was exciting but in a way that made her feel larger than life, as though she were the best possible version of herself.

Shaking her head at her fancy, she reached out for the sake carafe.

"I been a bad boy, mistress," slurred a voice behind her. It was the cowboy from earlier, looking a bit the worse for wear and more than a little drunk. "You should dis'pline me."

"Sorry, I'm off the clock," Trish said briefly, turning to glance back out at the Marquis.

"You're not dressed to be off'a clock. You're dressed to find a man, aren'cha," the cowboy said swaying, making her look at him again. "Well, I'm your man."

"I don't need one, thanks," she said with a forced laugh.

"'Course you need one." He moved close enough that she could smell the liquor on his breath.

The sushi chef had gone off to resupply, she realized. Though she heard music and the hum of conversation downstairs, the loft was empty. She searched for a way to shut him down but all the quick flippancy of her alter ego had suddenly deserted her. And the cowboy showed zero sign of going away. "I'm not looking for company," Trish said stiffly, trying to ignore the way he was staring at her breasts.

"Lissen to you. Oh, man, you're the kinda woman gets a guy right here," he said, grabbing his crotch. "You know, y'look so hot but then you just cut it off."

The effervescence she'd been feeling evaporated abruptly. Suddenly, she felt exposed in her scandalous party clothes. With confidence, they were high adventure; without, they merely made her vulnerable. She wished for a T-shirt, a sweatshirt, the loosest, biggest, bulkiest clothing she could find. She wished she were hidden, or a hundred miles away. Instead, she wrapped her arms around herself. "Look, I've got to go."

But he stood close, trapping her against the sake table. "Y'not gonna talk to me? Y' put on that li'l bit a nothin' and come on and then act like I shouldn' notice?" His voice rose a little.

She was in Sabrina's house, Trish reminded herself, and there was a room full of people downstairs. She was perfectly safe, she just needed to find a good way to end the conversation, and then leave. She kept her voice calm—strained, perhaps, but calm. "Look, I'm sure you're a nice guy," she began.

"I look atcha and I'm a walkin' hardon. I—"

"Are you ready to go look at that Warhol?" the Marquis asked from behind her. His fingers slipped around her elbow and Trish could have wept from relief.

"I'd love to."

"Excuse us," he said to the cowboy. Trish couldn't help noticing that he had several inches in height and a couple of inches in shoulders on the cowboy, who stared back at him in confusion. "I said excuse us," the Marquis repeated in a hard voice and Trish let him steer her to the stairs.

"Were we talking about a Warhol?" she asked in a low tone as they descended.

"No. You just looked as though you weren't particularly enjoying your conversation with Cowboy Bob, there. I figured I'd give you an excuse to leave if you wanted one. No, don't look up, he's still watching you."

"God," she said unsteadily, "I know how to pick 'em."

"I don't believe that was your choice." He turned at the living-room level and steered her down another half flight of stairs to the dining room. "In through here," the Marquis said, guiding her with a gentle touch in the small of her back.

They stood in the warm glow of Sabrina's kitchen, away from the music and the crowd. The caterers had set up in the garage, so for the moment all was quiet. The Marquis watched her as she leaned against the counter, rubbing her arms. "Something to drink?" he asked.

Trish looked at him blankly. Quickly, he began opening cabinet doors until he found tumblers.

"You shouldn't be going through her cabinets," Trish said faintly, but she accepted the iced water that he pressed on her.

"I think she'll forgive me."

The feel of the cold glass in her fingers made her shiver.

"Are you okay?" he asked. "What the hell did he say to you?"

Trish shook her head and took a deep breath. "Nothing much. It's okay." A woman like Delaney or Kelly would have told the cowboy to go to hell and gone about their business with no more than a passing thought. Why was it she'd never learned how? Don't think about it, she ordered herself, and with conscious thought dropped her hands back to rest on the edges of the counter at her sides. "Thanks for not making a scene."

"Fights tend to lead to broken furniture and unhappy hostesses," he said mildly. "I try to avoid them."

"You've been very nice."

"You make it easy." His eyes had glints of gold in them, she saw, as they looked back at her from behind the mask. The seconds stretched out. He cleared his throat. "There really is a Warhol over in the dining room. Do you want to see it?"

Trish gave a shaky laugh. "Sure."

"SO I NEVER KNEW Warhol did abstracts," Trish said, sitting on the kitchen counter and dangling her legs. "I just knew the pop art stuff." She took a drink of her water.

The Marquis had taken his frock coat off and tossed it over a chair in the breakfast nook. Now he leaned against the counter next to her. "Yep, Michelangelo gets remembered for the Sistine Chapel and old Andy gets soup cans and Marilyn Monroe. There's a legacy for you—soup."

"It could be worse," she explained, watching him roll up his sleeves over sinewy forearms. Watching him in his mask. "George Borden's claim to fame was evaporated milk."

"And then there was the toilet designer, Thomas Crapper—"

"Who we remember for obvious reasons," she finished with a laugh. It was good to be talking idle fool-ishness. The memory of the drunken cowboy was disap-pearing, replaced by the easy presence of the Marquis.

"I suppose it would be worthwhile to leave your name behind on something you did," he said thought-fully. "What would you want to be remembered for?"

"You first."

He pondered it. "Self-mowing lawns, I think. I'd gold plate my lawn mower and put it on a pedestal as yard art."

"Not big on yard work?"

"Summer afternoons should be for drinking beer and sitting in a hammock, not for going at the grass with a freakishly loud machine." He took a sip of his water. "And what about you?"

Watching him swallow scattered her thoughts for a moment. "Um, I don't know…never-ending hot water," she threw out.

"The endless shower?"

"Exactly. It would stay hot long enough for any-thing. You'd have time to condition your hair or scrub your back or…" The sudden visceral image of rubbing up against a slippery, soapy male body stopped her short.

She glanced up to find the Marquis's eyes on her. "Or?" he prompted.

"Just get really hot," she managed, then flushed. "I mean…" She cast about for conversation. "So how do you know Sabrina?"

His laughing eyes were trained on hers. "Oh, we've known each other since we were kids."

"Really? Does that make you another rich Hollywood baby?"

"Not at Sabrina's level. How do you know her?"

"College. We met working on a play."

"What was your role?"

Trish snorted. "Me, an actor? No way. I'm happier behind the scenes."

"You're center stage in that outfit."

"Don't believe everything you see." And she had to remember that she wasn't her alter ego, that she'd be going back to plain old Trish after the party was over. That she wouldn't have a sexy man dancing attendance on her and making her laugh.

"So what did you do on the play?" He pulled at his complicated cravat, untying it.

"Script doctor. You're losing your look, you know."

"Yeah, but I'm much more comfortable." He pulled off the cravat and unbuttoned the top buttons on his shirt so that she could see the strong column of his throat.

"I know, I know, image isn't everything." With his shirt loose he looked amazingly sexy, like the lord of the manor just before he set about seducing the scullery maid.

"Hello?"

She'd drifted off, Trish realized. "I'm sorry, what did you say?"

"Is that what you do now?" he repeated, rolling up his sleeves. "Write scripts?"

"In my dreams. I work for my sister. She's got a home concierge business. You know, grocery shopping, picking up dry cleaning, you name it."

"We do it all?"

"That was our old motto. Now it's Amber's Assistants: Servicing the Stars."

He laughed, seemingly before he could help himself. "Can't you get arrested for that?"

"I know, I know," she said ruefully, "but once Amber gets an idea in her head, she's hard to stop. Anyway, ever since the anesthesiologist from *Boston Memorial* signed on, she's been hot for the Hollywood vote."

"If you'd go to work dressed like that, Hollywood would probably be hot for you, too."

His appraising look made a little pulse of arousal surge through her. "Oh, yeah. I can just see myself dropping by the vet's office dressed like this."

"You could tell them you were doing a show."

She shrugged. "It's a living until I find something better. What about you? What do you do?"

"What do I do?" he repeated. "That's a good question."

"I know you're not a professional Marquis de Sade."

He studied her for a moment. "Well, it depends on how you define professional. Actually I—"

A sudden commotion came from the living room, and over it rose Sabrina's voice. "Okay, guys, show time. Everyone into the living room. *True Sex* is starting."

The Marquis looked at her. "I think we're being summoned."

All the party guests were clustered around the wide-screen TV. Trish might have been tall, and taller still in her heels, but in front of her rose a nearly impenetrable wall of heads and shoulders. She made a noise of frustration.

"Over here," the Marquis whispered, pulling her to the stairs across the room. "It's not close, but at least you'll be able to see something. Stand on the step." His hand was warm under her elbow, guiding her onto the stair. She felt an abrupt, fierce longing for a touch that was more than just a hug among friends.

And the documentary began.

Bare skin. Naked bodies. Unapologetic sexuality. Sabrina had vowed that her documentary was going to be something new and she was right. It wasn't cold and academic, it was natural, unguarded, often undignified.

And at times, completely and utterly erotic.

Trish watched the screen, but her awareness was focused on the man standing behind her. All she could think about was the heat, that magical warmth of another human body. She watched a couple take a lap dancing lesson, the man kissing his partner exuberantly at the end, and the wistful desire for the same kind of intimacy rose up in her. So many years, she thought, it had been so many years since anyone had touched her like that. She swayed lightly, hit by the sudden, intense need to lean back against the Marquis.

On the screen, the documentary switched to a couple playing with light bondage. "It's an incredible turn-on, when you know you can trust that person enough to let go," said a woman in a black peekaboo bra and G-string, holding hands with her partner. "I know I'm safe, I know if I say 'red,' everything stops. And it frees me up to let go."

"It's all about trust," agreed her partner, shirtless, in leather trousers. "It's about watching her body, seeing what turns her on and knowing when to stop."

On the screen, the woman lay on the bed and stretched her hands toward the bedposts. At the touch of the silk ropes, she shivered a little and stretched in arousal. "There's something amazingly erotic about just giving up control and worrying only about what I'm feeling," she said in voice-over as her companion trailed his fingers over her nipples. "I just let him take me away."

What would it be like, Trish wondered—no responsibility, no self-consciousness. No worry about what she was supposed to do. Bondage had always seemed like an alien concept but suddenly she could understand. A chance to just relax and abandon herself to the touch of a lover. A chance to thrill herself with the fantasy.

"Puts an interesting spin on it, doesn't it?" the Marquis murmured to her, curving his fingers around her shoulders and leaning so close she could feel the warmth of his breath.

An interesting spin, indeed, Trish thought. Suddenly she felt suffocated. She wanted out, she wanted air.

She wanted to be alone with him.

Without a word, she stepped around him and began to mount the stairs. She didn't have to look to see if he was following her.

She knew he would.

The night was clear, the sky speckled with stars, at least the handful that you could see in L.A. The rooftop was deserted. Trish walked to a corner and leaned on the concrete barrier to look out at the city lights. She felt the same anxiousness she did when on a roller coaster, just before the cars begin to rush headlong down the first drop.

The door clicked as he closed it behind him. Trish didn't turn, though she could feel his presence over her shoulder as he neared.

"Why the sudden rush to get outside?"

Trish shrugged. "It was stuffy in that room. I wanted some fresh air." She only waited a second before asking, "Why did you follow me?"

"Maybe there really is something amazingly erotic about giving up control. Don't you want to find out?"

In the humming silence, she turned to find him smiling at her, a wicked grin on his face. Somewhere deep inside, in some primitive part of her, a slow beat began to pound. "Take off your mask."

He leaned sideways on the barrier next to her and lightly stroked her bare arm with his fingertips. "I think it's better this way."

"What are you hiding?" She stared at his mouth, wondering what it would feel like on hers.

"Perhaps I'm a wanted criminal, laying low for the night."

"I'd almost believe that." Under his fingertips, her skin began to heat.

"Of course, that makes you my accomplice. What's your name, just so I know for the trial?"

"Trish." She shifted her body a bit toward his. "And yours?"

"Oh, I don't know, I kind of liked my lord."

"My lord?"

"Or master. Don't worry, I don't really get pleasure out of causing pain. Although I do have to confess to a certain fascination with my flail tonight," he added, running his fingers slowly through the strands as though absorbing the texture. "There's something about the feel of leather against bare skin that's incredibly hot." He stroked the strands of leather over her fingers. "Don't you think?"

Trish stared into his eyes, dark and unreadable, and shivered.

Then he moved his hand and ran the knotted leather straps over the soft, bare skin of her shoulder. "You're very sensitive there," he said softly. "You're shaking." He trailed the strands around the slender column of her neck.

She could feel herself tremble as she'd done earlier, in cold, in arousal, in excitement. He traced a finger where the leather had been.

Trish moistened her lips. "Take your mask off," she said quietly.

"But isn't it sexier for me to leave it on?" He set the flail aside. "Eyes without a face. The anonymous lover in the dark." He stepped closer and slipped his fingers into her hair. "It's so soft," he whispered. "That was the first thing I wondered when I saw you, how your hair would feel. And how it would be to kiss you."

Panic vaulted through her. She hadn't done this in a long time. She didn't remember how, wasn't sure she'd ever done it right to begin with. Being alone with him had seemed like a lark, but now she thought, no she was sure, it was a bad idea. Better to leave it as an unexplored possibility. Better to keep him from finding out who she really was. Better to end it now.

And then his lips touched hers, and thought whirled away, leaving only feeling.

So sweet. So warm. She hadn't remembered that a man's mouth felt like that. He didn't stick his tongue down her throat like the men—boys, really—she'd kissed before. He wasn't hurried and clumsy. Instead, he took his time, learning the shape of her mouth, sliding his hand over her cheek. It was undemanding and it made her relax. It was delicious and it made her savor.

Then he went deeper, taking her beyond enjoyment and making her want. When he sucked at her lower lip, she matched him; when he teased with the tip of his tongue she followed, suddenly eager to learn his flavors. It was half remembering, half finding her way beyond places she'd been before.

His hands slid down over her hips, warm against her. Earlier that night, she'd craved the feel of his body against hers. Now it was happening and she couldn't stop smiling. *Look at me,* she wanted to shout, *I'm kissing someone*. And what a someone.

The feel of his lips nibbling along her jaw and down her throat drew a small, incoherent sound from her. Then his mouth was on the tender skin of her upper breasts and all she could do was gasp. Something tugged in the center of her. This was what it felt like, she thought, this was what it was all about, this tempting, teasing touch that lured her, pulled her toward a door to some hot darkness where only sensation mattered. Half anxious, half impatient and wholly engaged, she closed her eyes and let her head fall back.

Only to feel a hard bolt of arousal shoot through her as he slid a fingertip under the edge of her bodice and brushed against her nipple. Blindly, she clutched at his hair and the wig slid to one side. With an impatient noise, he pulled it and his mask off, tossing them away even as he kissed her throat.

She wanted his mouth on hers, craved his taste, wanted him to drag her into that trembling haze of desire, that place she'd never felt before. When she heard his soft groan, she laughed against him exultantly.

And then he raised his head and Trish caught her breath. Shock flowed through her like ice water. She knew, suddenly, why his voice had sounded familiar. She knew why she felt so at ease with him. She knew his face, oh yes, she knew his face. Of course she did—she'd seen it fifty feet high in the movie theatre, and in smaller versions on television, in the newspaper, in magazines.

Ty Ramsay, action star extraordinaire.

Ty Ramsay, Sabrina's cousin, the fatally sincere heartbreaker.

"Jesus," she murmured.

And turned to bolt.

"Trish, wait." Ty reached the door at the same time as she did, cursing himself.

She stopped to face him, at bay. "What do you want?"

To understand what had just happened to him. To know how with a single kiss she'd pulled him in deeper than any woman he'd ever touched. To figure out why she looked absolutely panicked when she'd recognized his face. "Where are you going? Why are you so upset?"

"I'm not upset. I'm a little surprised, maybe," she said, her voice high and tense. "I get the whole mask thing, now. Sort of like the king dallying with the common folk."

"Or the alien living among the earthlings."

Even in the dark he could see her flushed cheeks. "Well, you can go back to your planet, now. It was fun and now it's done." She reached out for the door.

"Not as far as I'm concerned."

Trish gave a short laugh. "Sorry, this is as much as I do on rooftops in public."

But he'd caught a taste of something here that he wasn't about to lose. "Look, this felt right. Don't you want to see what happens next?"

"I think Sabrina's documentary showed you what happens next. There are books, in case you're confused."

Ty cursed impatiently. "I'm not talking about sex. We can just sit and talk for all I care." That wasn't precisely true. He was pretty sure he wanted more—much more—but for now he'd take another dose of their easy laughter. "Don't just run off. Please?"

Something flickered in her eyes—hope, maybe—and was quickly snuffed out by distrust. She reached behind her and opened the door. "Look, you're probably a really nice guy, but I'm sure you've got starlets to hang out with. Let's just call it good." Before he could react, she'd whirled and was gone, leaving only a trace of her scent in the air.

3

THE MORNING SUN was still close to the horizon as Ty Ramsay ran along the canyon trail. He moved with ease, his lean, rangy body springy with power, sweat gradually shading his dark-blond hair to brown. Plenty of people liked living in the Hollywood Hills or amid the hustle and bustle of the Wilshire Corridor, a heartbeat away from a power lunch. Ty had gotten over that. Living in the canyon was what worked for him now. His neighbors were the coyotes who lived down the hillside and the doves who nested in the eucalyptus, not the Hollywood elite. So maybe it took him a little longer to drive into town to meetings and parties. Then again, there weren't all that many parties worth being at anyway.

Except, maybe, for the one the night before.

Trish. He couldn't figure out why she'd hit him so hard. Sure, she was gorgeous. Sure, she'd been dressed to attract attention. Then again, he was surrounded often as not by beauties dressed to impress. There'd been something more about this one, something that had pulled at him. She didn't have the forgettable California blond look, but a delicate beauty that caught at his imagination, and an elusive wariness that made him wonder.

And brought her into his dreams.

It might have had something to do with their power-house kiss. It might have had more to do with laughing in the kitchen, watching the play of expressions over her face. Watching the stunned amazement writ large in the starlight as he'd trailed the leather of his whip over her shoulder.

His history with women had been checkered, at best. But he'd gotten tired of being a staple joke on the comedy circuit for having affairs with his costars. He'd made a vow nearly a year before to avoid relationships altogether until he figured out once and for all how to keep from making the same mistakes.

He had a feeling he was going to break his promise.

Ty followed the trail as it began winding back up the canyon. This early in the day, the October air held a crispness that gave him more energy as he went on, not less. The idea of body-sculpting in a glossy gym with some high-profile personal trainer did nothing for him. Better the peace and solitude of a morning run where the only noise was the thud of his footfalls and the whistle of an occasional bird. Ty glanced up at the walled house at the top of the hill, and sped up, knowing he was almost home.

Walls. Even in the canyon, you had to take personal security seriously, at least if you vied with Tom Cruise for top box-office draw around the globe. The little pulse of annoyance was so familiar he'd almost stopped feeling it. He'd known before he'd ever started acting what the price of fame could be, as he'd watched his uncle, Michael Pantolini, struggle with it. But when a college buddy had persuaded Ty to act in his senior project, everything had changed. Ty remembered the heady rush of those few short days, that sense of a previously unknown power surging through him.

He could no more have turned away from it than he could have stopped breathing.

And so he lived behind a wall and considered it a trade off. Ty slowed to a walk and turned down his asphalt driveway to see a bright-red Prius parked at the gate and a stocky, dark-haired man standing next to it, a camera slung around his neck. Speaking of privacy…

"Give us a smile for the hometown fans." The man gave a cocky grin, lifting the camera up to his eye.

"You know, the last paparazzi who tried to shoot me here were picking up their cameras in little pieces at the bottom of the hill," Ty told him, walking closer.

"No kidding?" The camera clicked and whirred as the photographer shot frame after frame.

"Once they finished picking *themselves* up, of course," Ty said pleasantly. "Want me to demonstrate?"

The intruder lowered his camera and smirked. "You ain't so tough."

"Try me," Ty suggested and took a step forward.

For a long moment they gave each other flinty-eyed stares. Then the intruder shook his head and waved the hand without the camera. "Cut."

Ty narrowed his eyes. "You directors, you're all alike. Never satisfied."

The "paparazzo" patted one of Ty's cheeks gently. "Ty, sweetie, you were fabulous, but if this goes any further you're gonna need a stunt double."

"You're just cranky because you're up on a Saturday before ten, Charlie."

Charlie snorted. "You forget I have kids. Eight o'clock is sleeping in."

Ty laughed and shook hands with Charlie Tarkington, college buddy and the person responsible for getting him into film. "I thought you hated leaving Santa Monica for the wilderness."

"I figured it was about time I brought your camera back."

"I was just going to put a call into the stolen property division. You could have gone through the gate, at least."

Charlie shrugged. "I forgot the code."

"It's the date of the premiere of our first movie, dork." Ty pressed his thumb on the security pad scanner and the gate glided noiselessly open to reveal the house beyond.

The structure was perched at the edge of the hillside. Sleek and white, the building's clean lines were banded with glass. The high wall might have been for the privacy a man in Ty's line of work had to fight for; the broad swathes of windows were for the freedom and openness he craved. When they stepped through the front door, it was to a flood of light, a room that stretched out and flung the viewer directly out into the canyon.

Charlie, as usual, went straight to the glass and stared out at the view. "You ever get nosebleeds up here?"

"Hey, when you make the big bucks you can afford

lots of cotton balls. Want something to drink?" Ty turned off into the kitchen to rummage in the refrigerator. He knew some actors who had cooks, maids, an entire staff to take care of them. So far, he'd resisted anything beyond a weekly housecleaning service and the occasional visit from a landscaping crew to keep the yard from getting too out of control. Outside, he was fair game for the public. Here, he jealously guarded his privacy. "What do you want, O.J.? Soda?"

Charlie wandered into the kitchen after Ty, idly surveying the brushed aluminum Sub-Zero appliances and granite counters. "I'm tempted to ask you for a cappuccino just for the entertainment value of seeing Mr. People's Choice Award figuring out how to use the knobs on that machine."

"For that, you get water," Ty said, grabbing two bottles from the refrigerator and tossing one to his friend.

Out on the deck, they relaxed in redwood Adirondack chairs and watched the morning mist burn away, until they could glimpse the sea in the bright distance.

"So, you into preproduction for *Dark Touch* yet?" Charlie asked idly, leaning back with a sigh.

"We start rehearsals next week."

Charlie turned his head to study Ty. "And you're not looking too thrilled about it."

"It's got problems, especially with the dialog." And unless Ty did something about it, he'd be the chump stuck mouthing the bad lines. "The concept's solid, it'll definitely play, but the script needs tightening."

"And?" Charlie prompted.

He shrugged. "And it's just another Ty Ramsay hero. You know, the strong, quiet outsider who comes in and saves the day against the terrorists or the mobsters or the counterfeiters or whoever. Same guy, different movie."

"They're not all the same."

"You're right." Ty gave a humorless smile. "They've each got their signature flaw: one smokes, one has anger management issues, one's a rule-breaker, one—"

"Dresses in women's underwear?" Charlie offered.

"Only in your movies. Admit it, Charlie, I've been one-tracked." Ty fell broodingly silent and stared out at the canyon.

"So ask your agent to get you some other kinds of scripts. Go for the dark, sensitive stuff."

If only it were that easy. "The studios want dark or sensitive they go to Nic Cage or Johnny Depp. They don't come to me. They come to me when they want a guy who's good at blowing stuff up." He took a long drink of his water and reminded himself he should be happy for his success, not feeling as though his life wasn't meshing the way he'd expected it to.

"Well, you could have the opposite problem. The studios look at me, they see Mr. Indie. Winning that jury prize at the film festival helped me in terms of getting small money, but it hasn't done dick for me in the big leagues."

"You want to blow stuff up?" Ty raised an eyebrow.

"Not exactly." Charlie took a pull on his bottle of water. "Just once, I'd like to do something that's not on a shoestring budget, though. If I could just have a crack at it, I could make it work."

"Don't I know that feeling. When you're talking about millions, though, they want to know you can do it before they put the money behind it."

"It bites," Charlie said moodily.

"Yeah."

They watched a swallow flit among the trees.

"You know—"

"Of course—"

They both stopped. "You first," Charlie said.

"What if we teamed up? To start a production company, I mean."

Charlie's eyes gleamed. "You took the words right out of my mouth. You act, I direct. With your name, we can find the financing. Hunt up a few scripts we like, start them into development…"

"Everybody's happy." Ty sat forward, suddenly alive with energy. "Equal votes. When we find one we both like, we go with it. Then later, once the company's running, we can pursue separate projects if we want."

"There's a script I've got optioned," Charlie said slowly, "but I haven't done anything with it because I know it would take more than I could come up with to do it right. I'll send it over to you Monday. If you're serious about this."

"I'm serious."

"Serious now or serious 'some day'?"

"Serious yesterday. I am so ready for this, you wouldn't believe." Ty lapsed into silence, drumming his fingers on the chair arm. "We'll need a name."

Charlie considered. "Two Guys Productions?"

"And you're supposed to be the creative part of the team? This is going to show up on a screen fifty feet high. How about Zephyr Productions?"

"Oh, sure, you want to name it after a bunch of hot air?"

"You've got a point," Ty allowed and thought some more. "Okay, how about GDI Films?"

"GDI Films? As in 'God-damn Independent'?"

"You know, that scrappy outsider thing."

Charlie mulled it over and nodded slowly. "It works. I like it. So what's our next step? We do the legal stuff, but how do we get things rolling?"

"I was at a party for the premiere of my cousin's doc the other night," Ty said thoughtfully. "Met a guy who might be good for coordinating things."

"As long as that's all he wants to do," Charlie warned. "We don't want to bring in some outsider who's going to try to run things."

"No, but we do need someone good to chase details. This guy sounds solid. I'll follow up, see if I can get more info on him."

"But keep it low-key." Charlie nodded his head to some beat that only he could hear. "So yeah, Sabrina's doc premiered last night, huh? How was it?"

"Really good. No surprise there. Sabrina knows what she's doing. And she gives a hell of a party." Trish, sliding her hand down her hip. Trish, dangling those delicious legs as she sat on the kitchen counter. Trish, silky and warm against him.

"So who is she?"

Ty blinked, then looked out at the canyon. "Sabrina's my cousin, you idiot."

"I'm not talking about your cousin. I know that look. Who is she? Tell Uncle Charlie."

Ty considered denying it, but Charlie always had been able to read him. "No one you know."

"I knew you wouldn't stay on the wagon," Charlie said comfortably.

"What's that supposed to mean?"

"Come on, even you, action boy, are human. You can say you're giving up women all you want, but you can only have so many gorgeous babes falling at your feet before you cave, right? Carpe diem and all that."

Ty gave him a narrow-eyed look. "Thanks for the vote of confidence."

"Hey, you're free, single and over eighteen. What's the problem?"

"I wasn't on the cover of the *Enquirer* once last year," Ty said, almost to himself. "It was kind of nice, you know?"

"You decided to give up women because of the tabloids?"

"No, I decided to take a break because I got tired of thinking I'd found the one and having it end in knockdown drag-outs with people I'd cared about."

The humor faded from Charlie's eyes. "Look, your parents, that love-at-first-sight thing? That doesn't happen to real people."

"So you keep telling me."

"And what you feel on a movie set when you're paid to pretend you're a guy in love with a knockout who's pretending to be in love with you, that's not real, either."

"Okay, okay." If Ty was sick of playing the same

parts in films, he was doubly sick of doing the same stupid things over and over again in his personal life. "Give me some credit, I've figured out the whole fooling-myself part. It's not all looks." There had to be more—a real connection, fun, complexity that made him want to get beneath the surface.

"So I take it this one's—er, what do we call her?"

"Trish."

"So this Trish looks like your grandmother, then?"

Ty's mouth tightened briefly, then relaxed as he saw the humor in it. "Not exactly."

"Didn't think so. Look, you have whatever fun you want, bud. Just don't let it interfere with GDI, because we've got a mission. GDI Films," he repeated. "I like it already."

SERVICING THE STARS read the blue-and-gold sign on the lobby wall of Amber's Assistants. Accurate, Trish supposed, if you counted a recurring bit character on the latest hospital drama as a star. Amber always had thought big.

The receptionist yawned and leafed through a magazine as Trish strode through the lobby and back to her sister's office. Amber sat there behind the polished oak desk, staring at her mouth in the mirror of her open compact while she outlined her lips with glossy red.

Tossing down a handful of labeled keys, Trish flopped into the client chair, wondering why Mondays always felt so hectic. "Tell me again why you pay Laurel to answer non-existent phone calls instead of getting her out to do some actual work like errands or appointments?"

Her sister shook back her mane of expensively maintained blond hair. "It gives us a professional look."

"I'm sure you could be just as professional and you'd save the cost of her salary."

Amber looked as though she'd been asked to clean the sewer. "I'm trying to run a business, here, in case you hadn't noticed," she said frostily. "Having Laurel frees me up to recruit new clients. For instance, Russell Nelson says one of his costars is looking for a personal assistant, and Russell's recommended us."

"Even so, how can you afford her?"

"I don't really think it's any of your affair, Trish. I'm the owner, and I say we can."

Trish didn't have the energy to get into it. "Look, the day's nearly over and I've still got four more things on my task list. You need another set of hands working, Amber. I can't do it all."

"The revenue won't support it."

Trish stared at her sister for a moment. Amber was, as always, serenely capable of maintaining a glaring contradiction. Six months before, when Trish had been newly laid off and unable to find another job, going to work for her sister had seemed like a good alternative to starvation. She'd help out with getting the business on its feet, pay the bills with a low-stress job and maybe finally finish that screenplay she'd always dreamed about.

It had only been once she'd started working that she'd remembered just how effectively she and Amber could drive one another crazy. Sisters, she thought with a sigh. The relationships defied reason.

Amber stared at her, eyes an impossible sapphire blue courtesy of colored contacts. "Look, you knew it wasn't going to be easy when you came on board. New businesses never are." She snapped shut her compact. "What do you have left to do?"

"If you could do the two dog feedings I've got left, I just need to drop off some groceries and deliver a pair of concert tickets."

"I suppose." Amber wrinkled her nose. "I hate that smell on my hands."

"You hate the smell? Did I tell you the Rizzettis' rottweiler yakked in my car?"

Surprise flickered for only a moment. "Well, you *were* taking it to the vet. You should have left it in the crate." Amber rose.

"You know my car won't take a crate that big. Next time, I'm taking your Xterra."

"Great. Then my car will reek, too."

Trish's smile wasn't entirely pleasant. "Welcome to my world."

"Don't start getting crabby. You're not qualified for the nutritionist or personal trainer jobs and you don't exactly dress like a personal assistant." Amber smoothed her fake Prada down over her size-four hips. "One of these days, Trish, you'll realize that appearance counts."

Oh, and didn't that just take her back to the bad old days of junior high, when she'd been a painfully shy fringe dweller still padded with baby fat. Big sister Amber was the kind of girl the Beach Boys had sung about, blond and tanned and bikinied, whereas Trish's

redhead's complexion had earned her only neon sun-
burns and a chronically peeling nose. Amber had been
the cheerleader, the homecoming princess, always at the
center of attention. In elementary school, Trish had na-
ively assumed that as she got older, she'd suddenly,
magically transform into Amber, surrounded by
bunches of popular friends, and sought after by the cute
boys.

Except that it hadn't happened that way. Instead,
she'd been an out-of-place loner most of the time. Getting a growth spurt and losing the baby fat the summer
after graduation hadn't changed things, either.

And college had taught her that thin women got their
hearts broken, too.

Well, she'd given up wanting to be the golden girl,
and image wasn't everything, no matter how much
Amber wanted to think so. Trish pushed back her un-
ruly curls. "Believe me, I didn't walk out of my house
today with this mop. It was an end-of-the-day treat,
courtesy of your plumber."

"Billy?"

"Yes, Billy. He didn't manage to get the faucet set
right."

"A leak?"

"More like a private version of dancing waters."

"Minus the music."

"Oh, no. He had Bon Jovi playing on KMET."

Amber fell into her infectious belly laugh that always came as a shock, and despite herself, Trish found
herself laughing along. And somehow, as so often happened, her irritation evaporated. With Amber, it was

never in the middle—Trish either wanted to strangle her or hug her.

Sisters, she thought with a sigh. Relationships with them definitely defied all reason.

TRISH PULLED HER MAIL out of the box and headed back across the courtyard toward her apartment, sorting through the envelopes as she walked. On the walkway ahead of her, a diminutive white-haired woman in a bright blue velour sweat suit tottered grimly along, pulling a wheeled carrier basket behind her.

Trish hurried up to her neighbor. "Let me get that. Ellie, why don't you let me shop for you?" she scolded. "You shouldn't be out running around when it's getting dark. I'm at the grocery store almost every day for work. It wouldn't take me any time at all."

"It's good for me to walk. I need the exercise." Ellie waved Trish off, but she surrendered the wheeled carrier basket to Trish quickly enough. "Besides, the Farmer's Market has some good end-of-the-day deals."

Trish lived in the oldest part of Park La Brea, within walking distance of the L.A. Farmer's Market and the L.A. County Museum of Art, not to mention the La Brea tar pits. She'd taken one look at the black-and-white tiled floors and the forties' ambiance of the apartment complex and fallen in love.

Back in her days of making a cushy salary at Focus PR, it had been easy to swing the rent. Now, she barely held on, spending her days running errands for Amber and her nights doggedly working on her screenplay meant that she was picking away at her savings all the while. She'd have to do something soon—like sell the screenplay or move somewhere cheap. For now, she pushed the thought out of her head.

Trish lifted the carrier basket over the threshold of Ellie's apartment. "Into the kitchen?" she asked, pushing her hair back over her shoulder.

"I'll get it from here, dear," Ellie instructed, pressing her hand. "You go work on your movie."

The problem, Trish thought later as she sat at her desk, was that work required concentration, and hers was currently shot. She was trying to tell the story of Callie, a woman who'd raised her younger siblings since she was eighteen. Now, ten years later, Callie watches them move into their own lives, finding herself simultaneously giddy and petrified at doing the same. She begins to spread her own wings; as she does she realizes that friendly, polite Michael McAdam down the street, the Michael McAdam she's known from a distance for years, harbors a romantic interest in her.

Trish's challenge was to add to the story, to take it from a small-time cable movie to a cinematic release. The key was Michael, who has loved Callie from afar and finally sees his chance with her. Michael has challenges of his own, though: a fugitive brother with mob ties, who puts Michael in the position of weighing family against morality and public censure—and the possibility of happiness with the woman he loves.

It all played itself out clearly in her mind. In her wildly optimistic moments, she imagined the story on the screen. The rest of the time she figured that just finishing it was enough, just doing what she'd always said she was going to.

And the finishing part was the challenge. She was trying to polish the lead-in to Callie and Michael's first kiss. The problem was that every time Trish tried to put herself in Michael's head and listen to his words, she kept hearing Ty Ramsay's voice. Every time she tried to imagine Michael's expression, she saw Ty Ramsay's face.

A clutch of butterflies chased one another in her stomach. For years, she'd imagined kissing someone again. The real thing hadn't even come close. It was just as well that Brett Spencer, the boy from college that she'd, well, *dated* certainly wasn't the right word. The boy who'd scalded her heart and humiliated her was, perhaps, more accurate, but that dignified it with more pathos than it deserved. He'd been a jerk, and a lousy kisser to boot.

The latter she could thank him for, not to mention the couple of guys who'd come later, because they'd kept her from knowing what she'd been missing. It would have been much harder to watch all the years go by if she'd had Ty's kiss to remember, she thought, touching her fingers to her lips.

Enough, she told herself, blowing a strand of hair out of her eyes. She had a whole weekend to write and a draft of a screenplay that needed revisions. The polishing was key, polishing she wasn't going to get done if she spent the entire time mooning around over a kiss that said guy had probably forgotten ten minutes after it had ended. First things first, she needed to get her hair out of her face; then she could tackle the rest.

Trish searched under the papers on her table until she uncovered the oversized hair clip that she knew was there. With an impatient huff, she piled her hair up on her head and fastened it in place. There. One distraction out of the way. As to the other distraction, a little discipline would take care of that.

Old Dire Straits played in the background and she began to type. At first, the words came to her in fits and starts, then she started to become immersed. Slowly but surely, the lines started to fill the computer screen, making her smile.

The buzz of the telephone shattered the calm. Trish reached out for the receiver. "Hello?"

"It's Ty Ramsay."

And in an instant, Trish was slammed back to Sabrina's roof, to starlight and the taste of Ty's lips, to the feel of his hands. Nerves vaulted through her. "How did you get my number?"

"You left way too quickly the other night."

Trish swallowed, searching for her composure. If she were smart, she'd stay a million miles away from him. She'd heard all of Sabrina's warnings, and anyway, she should have learned her lesson from Brett Spencer. Guys like Brett and Ty lived in a different world and someone like Trish would do well to keep that in mind. But oh, she couldn't forget the heady wonder of the party, that sense of every moment existing in a wash of golden light. "I seem to remember saying goodbye."

"Not to Sabrina. She was looking for you."

"Yes, I know." She'd already been grilled by Sabrina and Cilla, both. Fortunately, her long-standing reputation as the group party pooper made her early departure easy to explain. Or, depending on how Ty had come to call her, maybe it hadn't. "Did Sabrina give you my number?"

Ty laughed. "No. I have my ways of getting information. It helps to be connected in Hollywood."

"I suppose." She crossed over to her sofa.

"So we never did resolve that immovable object paradox."

"It's not a paradox if the irresistible force and the immovable object don't meet," she said, sinking down into the cushions.

"Well, we definitely met. You can't deny that."

And she felt the little tug in her stomach just thinking about it. "Yes, but the irresistible force and the immovable object are separated now, so there's nothing to resolve."

"Oh, I think there is. And I definitely think we should discuss it further. In person."

Trish took a breath. "Thanks for asking, but I told you last night, I'm not interested." She'd be out of her mind to get involved with him, however much she might be tempted.

"Well…we had a good time, until you realized who I was. So, I don't know, should I go back to wearing the mask and wig? Would you go out with me then?"

She laughed despite herself and put her feet up on the coffee table. "I can just see it now, you wearing the mask into the Sky Bar. The paparazzi would love it."

"Better yet, you could come to my house. That way, we'd actually get some privacy."

"I'm sure," she said dryly. No way was she going into the lion's den.

"I'll be a complete gentleman, I swear. You can borrow my whip and discipline me if I get out of line."

She traced a little pattern in the plush green fabric of the couch. "I'm not trying to be rude. I just don't see it working."

"It seemed to be working last night."

How could she be any clearer than that? What did it take? And why couldn't she make herself take it to the next level and tell him to take a hike?

"Look," she tried, "I'm really not trying to be difficult. You're just…out of my league." And she needed to remember it.

"Why, because of my job?"

She gave a short, humorless laugh. "You're the only person I can think of who would refer to being world-famous as a job, but yes, that's part of it. You're a G-boy. You're…I don't know, too big a star. Too good-looking, too rich." She made a noise of impatience. "I don't run in your circles and I'm not going to try."

"So, basically, what you're telling me is that if I were homely and worked at a convenience store you'd go out with me?"

Trish couldn't suppress the smile. "I'd think about it."

"I could get plastic surgery," he offered. "That would take care of the looks. Probably the job, too, now that I think about it," he reflected.

"You can't be that hard up for a date."

"No, I'm not. And that should tell you something right there."

"Yes it does." Suddenly, she was tired of being backed up against a wall. "It tells me that you're one of these guys who gets off on the challenge. I don't want to be your latest hit-and-run, thanks very much."

There was a short silence. "Sounds like you've been talking with Sabrina."

"What if I have? Don't say none of it happened, because the newspapers say differently."

"And of course they never lie. Look, maybe I haven't always been an angel, but it's the past. It's not what happens now."

"Yeah, well, the only way I spend time with people I don't want to is when I'm getting paid for it."

"I'll see what I can do."

She snorted. "Goodbye, Ramsay."

"Bye-bye, cupcake."

4

"'MORNING, LAUREL," Trish said as she walked through the lobby of Amber's Assistants. If only writing were her full-time job. Briefly, she indulged in a fantasy of walking in and giving notice to Amber. *It's been a slice and thanks for the memories, but you're making me crazy and I quit.*

Heaven.

Bliss.

And not likely to happen any time soon unless the job market recovered or she sold her script, she thought with a sigh, remembering her bank balance. Time spent in wishful thinking was time wasted. The screenplay was never going to sell unless she finished revising it and showed it to an agent. What she needed was to grab her task list and get to work so that she'd have some time and energy to write at the end of the day.

"Be sure to stop in Amber's office," Laurel called after her. "She wants to see you."

It wouldn't truly be a workday without a run-in with Amber, Trish thought resignedly. She stopped in the room where they kept the assignment lists and keys, then walked down the hall to knock on Amber's open door. "Hi. You wanted to see me?"

Amber looked up from her computer. "Have a seat." Her voice was strung tight with excitement or frustration or something Trish couldn't quite decode. There was no point in trying to figure out what to expect. Amber was one of a kind.

Amber finished tapping on her keys and turned toward Trish. "So you didn't think we could live up to servicing the stars, did you?" she said without preamble.

"Amber, it sounds like the motto for an escort agency." Trish kept her voice mild.

Amber flushed. "It sounds fine. You just think it's a silly goal."

Patience, Trish told herself, and managed a casual shrug. "It's your business, it's up to you to decide, but take a look at your books. You've got a solid client roster. You're making money. Who cares if you don't have a bunch of Hollywood bozos coming to you?"

"Who says I don't?"

"Have Hollywood bozos?" Trish thought of Mr. B-list Russell Nelson. "Not me."

"Ha, ha. Well, you can stop looking down your nose. Our Hollywood roster just got bigger."

"Really? That's great," Trish said, genuinely pleased for her. She might have her doubts about Russell and his buddy, but Russell did pay his bills, even if his demands were somewhat self-indulgent. "I'm happy for you, Amber. I'm sure it's the start of big things. We'll have to go celebrate." She tapped her fingers restlessly. "Was that all? Because I've got a full schedule today so I should get rolling."

"Actually no, you don't." Amber flicked a glance at her.

"I don't what?"

"You don't have a full schedule. Forget the errands, I'm shifting you over to personal assistant."

Trish blinked. "Okay, not three days ago you were telling me I wasn't qualified for anything but dog-walking. Now I'm a personal assistant? What gives?"

Amber opened up a file, her posture rigid. "Our new client is looking for a personal assistant. I've chosen you."

The way she bit off the final sentence made Trish wary. "And who, exactly, is our new client?"

Amber flashed a triumphant smile. "Ty Ramsay."

"Oh, hell," Trish said.

Hell, indeed. She had only herself to blame, yapping away to Ty about her work. Apparently all she'd accomplished by putting him off was to make him more determined. Well, she had news for Mr. Superstar. She wasn't ridiculously flattered that he'd tracked her down. She wasn't. Not a bit. Really. It was all about ego for him, anyway. He figured he could just pull on a few strings and like a little puppet she'd do his bidding.

He figured wrong.

"I'd expected you to be more excited for me." Amber gave her a chilly look. "This is huge, Trish."

"No argument here. That's why I think you should be the one to work with him. You'll make a more professional impression." Feed her vanity, Trish thought. Do whatever was necessary to stay away from Mr. Ty Ramsay. Mr. Heartbreaker Ty Ramsay. What had Sabrina said? Fatally sincere? Right. "You take the job, Amber," she urged. "You're more his type."

"I don't think it has anything to do with type," Amber said frostily. "I would do a better job. You're right, but I'm going to give you a chance." The look on Amber's face would have curdled milk. There was no way the arrangement was voluntary. "So just when, exactly, did you start running around with the likes of Ty Ramsay?"

Trish's gaze cooled at her tone. "He was at Sabrina's party last Friday. We talked." *And he kissed me senseless.*

"You hung out with Ty Ramsay?" Amber gave her a patronizing smile. "Are you're sure you're not exaggerating a little bit?"

It got Trish's back up. "Why is that such a shocker? I do socialize, you know."

"Oh, sure. Well, it must have been some socializing if he wants you for an assistant. What did you tell him, anyway?"

I told him no. "Nothing. We just talked a little in passing."

Amber stared at her, a little frown creasing her brow. "Well, I don't see what that has to do with him wanting you for a personal assistant," she said finally.

"Nothing." Trish had had enough. She rose to walk out. "Tell him you're the only one who can do it."

"I already did," Amber snapped. "He said it's you or he goes elsewhere. So it's you."

Trish stopped and turned. "No," she said with a calm she didn't feel.

"No?" Amber's expression went tight with incredulous fury. "I gave you a job when you were unemployed. I've kept you working, and now, when the chance comes for you to do something to keep this business going, you're refusing?"

"Amber, I've been working fifty-hour weeks for you on this job so that you could cut staff," Trish protested. "You couldn't have kept it going without me."

"Don't start with me, Trish," Amber hissed. "You want me to bring out the big guns, I will."

Translation: a call to their mother. "Didn't we get over tattling in junior high?"

Amber's lips were white with anger. "You are not going to screw this up for me, understand?"

What had she been thinking by going to work for Amber? Trish wondered, stomach roiling. She should have had her head examined. Any other job, she could just quit. If she walked away from this one right now, she'd never hear the end of it, from Amber or their mother.

Ty Ramsay had her well and truly trapped.

She consciously loosened her jaw and took a breath. "Okay, fine, I'll do it. How long?"

"He's faxed a six-month contract."

"I'll do it for three. That should give you enough time to arrange a substitute." And give her time to polish up her résumé.

"Thanks for that sacrifice." Amber's voice was without heat. "You'll work out of his house. Be there today, 10:00 a.m."

"Out of his *house?*" Trish's voice cracked.

"What's your a problem here, Trish?"

"Look, you've got what you wanted," Trish said, biting down on her anger. "Let's leave it at that."

"Fine. Here's the address." Amber held out a slip of paper. "You should get going. Don't be late."

"Fine." Trish collected the directions and turned to go.

"And Trish?"

She stopped at the door and looked back.

"Put on something besides a T-shirt and jeans, for God's sake."

TRISH DROVE NORTH on Pacific Coast Highway, headed toward Latigo Canyon Road. The glinting sea on her left and the puffy clouds in the blue sky overhead did nothing to improve her mood. She'd put on something besides a T-shirt, Trish thought defiantly, fingering the fleece of her hooded blue sweatshirt. Ty Ramsay thought he wanted her around? Wait until he saw the real her. She had a funny feeling his demand for a six-month contract would fade as quickly as one of his grand passions.

And she could get back to getting him out of her system.

Her irritation carried her all the way up the winding canyon, to the driveway that led to Ty's house. She turned in and stopped for a moment, taking a deep breath. There was no reason to be nervous, she told herself. Five minutes would take care of this little fiasco. She'd show up, he'd cool off, and that would be that. Game over.

She drove up to the gate, stopping at the little speaker to press the call button.

"Hello?"

Her stomach jumped at the sound of his voice. "It's Trish Dawson from Amber's Assistants."

"Hey. Come on in." The gate slid noiselessly back.

No way was she going to be impressed by the clean lines of the white house, or by the sweeping views to either side. She studiously ignored both, driving onto a broad concrete parking apron edged with hibiscus. Taking a deep breath, she turned off the ignition and got out of the car. He might have charmed her at Sabrina's party when she didn't know who he was, but that wouldn't happen now. She knew enough to be wary of him. There was no way he was going to get on her good side.

Then Ty Ramsay walked out his front door wearing a denim shirt untucked over jeans, looking as artlessly perfect as though he were in a shot in a movie. The sunlight brought out glints of gold in his hair. His eyes, as he approached, were the color of drift glass. "Good morning."

She'd seen him on the screen and in magazines, but always at a distance. His was a face made for the camera: straight nose, cleft chin, clean jaw, a mouth that could hold both strength and tenderness. Looking at him, though, she didn't see the individual features. She saw a careless charisma in the intelligence and flickers of fun in his eyes, backed with enough sexuality to blast the top of her head off.

Trish grabbed at her irritation as though it were a

lifeline that might keep her from being swept away. "You really don't take no for an answer, do you?" she asked as she stalked up to him.

"That was dinner. You never said anything about work."

"Don't split hairs. You knew what I meant."

"I needed an assistant," he said easily.

Without the benefit of high heels, Trish had to tip her head to stay eye to eye with him. "And you just happened to pick Amber's Assistants out of all of the businesses in the city?"

"It did start with the letter *A*," he said reasonably. "But no, I just happened to pick Amber's Assistants because I knew you worked there. And I wanted to see you again."

What was she supposed to do when a man that heartbreakingly gorgeous said something like that to her? Even though she knew she couldn't trust him, even though she knew the last thing in the world she wanted was to go anywhere near him, the pleasure in his eyes looked so genuine. *Fatally sincere.* Trish was certain she could smell her synapses frying.

Ty just watched her steadily, a little smile playing over that mouth, with its little depression in the bottom lip that made it look as if he was just about to taste something really wonderful.

And she remembered when that something had been her.

Trish shook herself mentally. "Well, you've seen me. Satisfied?"

"Careful using a word like that when your motto's Servicing the Stars."

The corner of her mouth twitched.

"But you've already made it clear that that's not an option." He tipped his head consideringly. "'Course, I figure I've made some progress just by having you here."

"This is not a date," she reminded him.

"Don't blame it on me. I tried."

This time she did smile a little, with an uneasy sense that she was losing her grip on the situation. "I'm here to work."

"Trust me, you will." He reached out to take her satchel. "Let's go inside and I'll show you the setup."

As she stepped through the door onto the marble tiles of the entryway, Trish had to struggle not to stare. The living room alone would have held her whole apartment. What seemed like an acre of celery-colored carpet stretched away toward a wall of windows that opened out on the canyon. A waterfall in the entryway sent a sheet of water down rough slate to drip into a catchment basin, filling the space with the tranquil sound of flowing water. The furniture was distressed leather, dotting the room in comfortable groups. A painting hung opposite her, a few slashes of color that somehow managed to suggest the space and openness of the desert at sunset.

The room held a sense of calm that surprised her. She wouldn't have expected superstar Ty Ramsay to live in a space like this. Then again, she wouldn't have expected Ty Ramsay to live so far outside of town.

A tasseled silk rope hung over the arm of a couch that faced out toward the windows. On the coffee table lay the Marquis's whip. Trish felt her pulse speed up as she fingered the silk. She turned to look at him. "So is there something I should know about here?"

"That? Oh, I'm breaking in a new sex slave." He kept a straight face for a beat, then broke into laughter. "It's from my current project," he explained. "We're in rehearsals. I figured a few props would help me get into my character's head."

"So that's why you were dressed up at Sabrina's party?"

"Dipping my toe in the water," he agreed.

Trish looked at him warily. "Don't even tell me you hired me to help you out with your toe-dipping."

"Well, you're my assistant. I thought…"

"You go to hell, Ramsay," she snapped. "You wanted someone for fun and games, you should have flipped to another section of the phone book." She turned to leave and he caught at her arm.

"Hey, take it easy. I was only joking."

Face flaming, she shook off his arm. "I know," she muttered.

Ty studied her. "So why are you so jumpy? I don't bite."

"I'm not jumpy."

He resisted the urge to smile. She wore an unzipped sweatshirt over a red tank top and jeans. Her hair was a tumbled mass flowing over her shoulders, not the smooth, sophisticated spill it had been at the party. In her face, he read nerves, tension and, most of all, defiance.

"I'll take your word for it. The computer and phone

are right here." He'd had to make some fast phone calls that morning to get another computer in time, but it was instructive how much a person could get done with a little charm and deep pockets. He'd wanted Trish there, and if it took buying furniture and a computer to make it happen, it was little enough to do.

Trish walked over to rest a hip against the polished maple table that held the sleek iMac. "So why don't you tell me what you're expecting me to do?"

He couldn't keep himself from studying the hollows at the base of her neck. When he'd met her, she'd been dressed to show off those sexy eyes, that fabulous body. Now, she was dressed to hide them. It didn't make sense, and it didn't work a lick because her face still fascinated him.

And the riddle of her fascinated him even more. "What do I want you to do? Whatever comes up. Run errands, make arrangements for me, pay bills. Simplify my life."

"Does your life need simplifying?"

He grinned. "Doesn't everyone's?"

"Why don't you have an accountant pay your bills?"

He shrugged. "I remember reading when I was a kid about this legendary basketball star waking up one morning with nothing because his accountant embezzled it all. I figured if I ever made a lot of money, I'd sure as heck know what was happening to it."

"I thought you came from a big-money Hollywood family," she objected.

"I was raised thinking that you made your own way." He smiled faintly. "You look surprised. I didn't use my family to get ahead, you know, or to pay my way."

"Most people would."

"Family's supposed to be there for you, not do everything for you. If I succeeded, I wanted to know I'd done it myself." And it was worth all that work to watch the respect creep into her eyes.

"You're different than I expected you to be," she said finally.

"Expectations will confound you every time."

She moistened her lips and took a brisk breath. "So, um, you want to keep your own hands on your money. We can set up a lot of your everyday bills to autopay, though. Utilities, mortgage, that sort of thing."

"See, I knew from the moment I laid eyes on you that you'd make my life better."

"You're easily impressed," she tossed out.

"No," he smiled, "I'm not."

5

AFTERNOON SUN slanted in through the windows. Trish sat at the computer, ostensibly typing a letter but mostly trying to ignore Ty. He was sprawled on the couch, idly running the silk rope through his fingers as he read the script that lay open in his lap. His eyes were intent, his mouth firm in concentration. Something about the way he stroked the rope made it impossible to keep from glancing at him. Then he looked up without warning and caught her watching. Trish started typing furiously, face burning. Out of the corner of her eye she saw his mouth curve in amusement.

"Let me know if you're looking for something to do," he said, a hint of laughter in his voice.

"I'm fine, thanks," she replied.

He flicked an appreciative glance at her. "You are, you know."

Before she could react, he lapsed back into silence, tossing the silk rope aside. Picking up the flail, he slapped the leather thongs lightly against the couch, absorbed in reading the script.

Trish tried to ignore the pattering swack of leather hitting leather. *Focus,* she told herself and printed out the letter. A moment later, she picked up the phone to call in an appointment for him. There was something alarmingly intimate about scheduling him for the dentist, about writing out checks for him to sign to pay his bills. She'd hoped that her initial nerves would abate into detachment; instead, as the day had worn away, they'd eased into a dangerous comfort.

The rhythmic noise of the flail was louder now, and more impatient. Finally, Ty cursed and stood up, tossing the whip aside.

"You need something?" Trish asked.

"Yeah." He walked over to her. "A script writer who has a clue about the way people really talk."

"What?"

He shook his head. "Never mind. I just need a highlighter and some sticky notes."

Slapping the open script down on a corner of the desk, Ty reached in front of her to pull open the drawer under the work surface. Sudden alarm vaulted through her. Had she said comfort? Yeah, right. Maybe when he'd been safely across the room, but this close to him, *comfort* was the last word that applied.

He'd rolled up his sleeves. His forearms were tanned and strong, and those hands—she could imagine him building fine furniture, running those long fingers over exotic wood grain, polishing it until it was silky smooth.

She could imagine his hands on her skin.

Trish jolted as Ty's arm brushed against her. His mouth was close enough to kiss she thought as he leaned over her. She could smell that elusive scent of soap that hung around him. Her breath hitched.

"I thought you said you weren't jumpy," Ty said, his eyes meeting hers.

"I just wasn't expecting…" Her voice trailed off and she groped desperately for something to say.

"What?" he asked softly. She could see the gold flecks in his blue-green eyes as they focused on hers, she could almost taste his mouth. It would take so little for him to close the gap.

And she was afraid of how much she wanted him to.

The phone rang, rescuing her. Trish cleared her throat. "I'll just get that, shall I?" Her voice was brisk. "Let's see, you said if they're not on the list, take a message, right?"

Ty looked at her for a long second, then grinned and straightened. "Sure. I'll be in the kitchen if it's anyone I need to talk to."

Trish let out a breath and picked up the receiver. "Hello?" She listened to the caller for a moment. "Just give me a moment and I'll see." She punched the hold button. "Ty? It's your agent."

He reappeared from the kitchen with two glasses of water. "I'll trade you," he said, and took the cordless phone from her. "Hey, Maureen, how're you doing?"

Trish sipped her water and began working on paperwork she'd downloaded to set up autopayment on Ty's bills, even as he walked out of the room talking points and grosses. She put a great deal of concentration into filling out forms for him to sign, setting them in a neat pile on top of the invoices. Unfortunately, it was simple work that didn't do nearly enough to distract her from the white blur in her peripheral vision. The white blur that was the screenplay.

She really ought to mind her own business. Ty's script wasn't her affair. If she was going to worry about screenplays, she had an unfinished one sitting at home that could use her attention. Trish uttered another oath as she realized she'd written her own name instead of Ty's on a form and slapped down her pen.

Okay, okay, okay. She was only going to take a glance. It wasn't like she was actually prying. He'd left it open right under her nose, after all. And she was trustworthy. She wasn't going to run off and plagiarize it or spill it to the tabloids or anything. She was just going to take a peek. A harmless little peek.

The script told the story of an FBI agent tracking a killer through the world of dominance and submission. Navigating that world, she becomes enthralled with a dominant who is possibly the murderer. He leads her into the world of bondage and submission, a world of alarming fascination.

In places, especially toward the end, when the FBI agent and the dominant teamed to find the real villain, the story vaulted along and Trish couldn't turn the pages fast enough. In others, it lurched along and very nearly collapsed under its own weight. She could see why Ty was frustrated.

It didn't register to her that she was rewriting it in her head as she skimmed the pages, mentally revising the dialog, the pacing, the flow. The bones were good; it was just the flesh layered on top that was problematic. How to fix it was clear. If the heroine just said—

"Interesting reading?"

Trish jumped at the sound of Ty's voice behind her. "I'm sorry. It's not what it looks like. I was just…I mean, I thought…" She floundered, looking for the right thing to say and then huffed in impatience. "It was right here. I couldn't resist looking."

He replaced the cordless phone in its cradle and studied her. "That's right, you're a script doctor, aren't you?"

Her pulse jumped. "Hardly. I mean I was in college, but what's that worth?"

"What's the worth of this writer's track record as a paid screenwriter?" Ty countered.

"He knows his stuff. He's got the pacing and the story. There are parts that flow just fine." Her voice steadied as she gained confidence.

"It's the other parts I'm worried about."

"You're right, some of those lines don't sound like anything a real person would say."

"Exactly. And I'm the real person who's got to say them."

"Can you get them to take another crack at it?"

He shook his head. "Been there, done that. Trust me, it's better than it was before the first revision."

"But not good enough."

"Not by half. Like you said, Trish, he tells a good story, it's just the dialog that doesn't work."

"Sometimes it does." She began flipping through the pages she'd read. "This part here, where he's showing her around the club, this part is dead on."

"True. But the next scene, where they walk into the back is dead off. I mean, my character sounds like a pretentious pinhead."

"Pinhead?"

His lips twitched. "Yeah."

She dragged her eyes away from his mouth. "Well, it could be a good career move. You know, help you get out of being typecast?"

"That I could use. I just don't think that pinhead is the direction I want to go in," he said dryly.

"I don't think it's that bad, really." She skimmed the lines. "Look, up to right here where he invites her to sit and talks about pleasure and pain, it works."

"Ah yes, the 'pleasure and pain divide.' Give me a break."

"Yeah, but what about if you change it? Have him move in on her slowly, sort of hypnotically, asking her if she's ever felt ice so cold it was hot, that it's all about the point where the senses break down, where pleasure becomes pain and pain becomes pleasure. That's what you want, for him to be drawing her in so that she gets fascinated by the lure and doesn't realize the danger underneath. Or maybe she doesn't care," Trish added almost to herself. Opening up a file in the computer, she began tapping out lines of dialog, her fingers a blur of motion. "Like this, see?"

She didn't notice that Ty was studying her almost as much as the screen.

"And he's pulling her in just to amuse himself, although he starts to get in deeper than he expects as it goes forward. And that puts him in danger, eventually, I'm guessing." She glanced up to find Ty way too close to her. Her heart began thudding. "Or something like that, right?"

"Oh, yeah, you're dead on," he said slowly. "The script doesn't play it quite like that, but it should."

"He's pretty ambiguous for the first half of the film." She slid her fingers restlessly over the keys. "It's a little bit of a departure for you."

"Not nearly enough of one."

"But still, it's different."

"I don't mind different. I'm kind of looking forward to it, actually. What I mind is when the character doesn't work. Can you print out those pages you just typed? And then keep going, if you want to. I'm curious to see your take on it."

"Just for kicks, right?"

"Just for kicks," he agreed, scooping the pages up out of the printer and crossing to the couch.

The only thing she liked better than writing was editing. Trish pulled a line out of the script and followed where the conversation led in her head, hammering out the interchange as quickly as she could type. Finally, at the end of the scene, she stopped. The printer hummed and Trish stretched as the pages slid into the hopper. "Here's the rest," she said, carrying the sheets of paper over to Ty.

It made her nervous, wondering what he was going to think. She perched nearby to watch him read.

Ty lapsed back into silence. Seconds passed, then minutes. Finally, he stirred. "So how set are you with the part in the couch?"

Trish blinked in surprise. "Um, not at all. I mean, I don't think it's mine to be set on anything. This is just for fun, Ty. You're not actually going to take this in, are you?"

"Why not? It works." He looked up. "Unless you don't want me to. I have script input rights on this one, and I'd see you got paid."

She ruthlessly suppressed the little thrill it gave her. "I don't know, I'd rather not have a guild screenwriter looking for my head on a platter."

"You kidding?" Ty snorted. "Scripts get revised all the time. They may not like it but they're used to it. Dale Westhoff, the director, is real clear on his blocking for the scene, though, so whatever changes I bring in need to work within that."

Adrenaline rushed through her. It was a chance, a real chance to do something. "What's he got for blocking?"

"I'll need you to stand in for the actress."

"Okay."

Ty rose. "So they've walked into his office and he's offered her a seat while he gets drinks. The whip and the rope and stuff is out, and she's caught up in looking at it while he's off at the bar." At his gesture, Trish picked up the silk rope. "Good. Now here's where he had that whole line about the pleasure-pain divide thing as he's handing her the glass of ice water, and then he talks about making her nerve endings come alive with the ice cube." He gave a pained look and sank down on the couch beside her. "We ditch the line, but we've got to have a lead-in to using the ice. Dale's really hot on it."

She swallowed. "It works fine with the new dialog. That's where he can be talking about something so cold it feels hot. Take it one more step, have him actually get an ice cube and rub it on her skin." Following the script notes, Trish lay back on the pillows propped against the arm of the couch.

"Yeah, but the part where he says 'The edge draws you, I can see it,' is where he slips the rope around her wrists and then kisses her. Totally wooden. How can we work that into your stuff?"

"Again, fix the dialog and the scene will fix itself. Skip the 'drawn to the edge' stuff and have him say something like 'don't you wonder what it's like out there, beyond where it's safe? Don't you want to try it?' and have him tease her with the rope."

"Like this?" Ty asked, moving beside her to trail the satiny tassel over the bare skin above the neckline of her tank top.

Trish shivered. "Yes. And he sees her reacting, he knows how to manipulate her sexually and emotionally because he's done it to woman after woman, and he says—"

"'You'd try it if you knew you could be safe, wouldn't you?'" Ty's voice was husky.

Trish let out a shuddering breath. "And she says 'yes.'"

Ty slowly tied the silk rope around Trish's wrists, binding them together. "And is she scared here, or curious?" His eyes were intent on hers.

"Both," Trish whispered as he pulled her hands up over her head and held them in place against the back of the couch. The slippery softness of the silk against her skin made her shudder; having her hands bound, however cursorily, was immensely erotic. The air felt cool against her skin.

Ty leaned toward her, until his lips hovered just a fraction above hers. "So he says 'you are safe with me.'"

"And she says 'I don't believe you,'" Trish managed. Her lifeline was long gone, she had nothing to keep herself from slipping into dangerous depths.

She knew it was foolish. She didn't seem to be able to help herself.

"'I don't think this is smart.'" She wasn't sure whether these words were hers or not.

His eyes were very green up close. "'We're well beyond smart.'"

"'I shouldn't be doing this.'" Trish's words were barely audible.

"'You want it anyway,'" he whispered.

And his mouth claimed hers.

The kiss wasn't soft and easy, like the first time. It was hard, urgent, drawing her down into a churning whirlpool of sensation. This time wasn't about exploration, it was about knowing where they were going, knowing how it would be.

Trish moved to touch him. Her wrists pulled against the rope and a little lick of arousal whipped through her. Bound. Tied. Ravished. His tongue tantalized hers and she moaned. His fingers traced the band of skin exposed where her tank top had ridden up and she craved it. She wanted more, his hands hard against her, on her breasts, stroking down her sides, touching her everywhere.

Her gasp was loud in the quiet of the room.

Trish pulled her wrists apart involuntarily and the rope, already loose, unwound, freeing her hands to slip down into Ty's hair. Part of her missed the thrill, part of her savored the feel of his muscles under the shirt as her hands slid lower. She wondered what he would feel like naked, how it would feel to have only bare skin under her fingertips.

She wondered if she'd ever have the nerve. Perhaps she should just stick with his divinely decadent kisses, but that wasn't possible because she knew there was more and she wondered just where it would take them. She wondered—

The phone shrilled in the background. For a moment, they both froze as though part of some tableau of decadence. Then it shrilled again and Trish jolted.

Ty raised his head. "I keep meaning to turn that damned ringer off," he muttered.

Trish sat up, raking her hair off her face. "Oh, I don't know, I think it's a useful reminder," she said, dropping the rope in his lap.

The answering machine picked up and the voice of his agent filled the room. Ty swore pungently and got up off the couch. "I'd better get this."

Trish resisted the urge to bang her head against the coffee table. She should have seen that one coming a mile away. Then again, maybe she had seen it and just didn't care because the man kissed like a god. That was it. That was what she felt like, one of those maidens in Greek mythology who got seduced by a deity who'd come down to Earth in the guise of a mortal or a swan.

Enough of the flights of fancy. The fact was that she'd let herself get overheated and overexcited, and now she'd gotten into something with a client. A *client*.

This time, she did bang her head. A deep breath worked better, though.

After all, there were facts at work here. Fact number one, there was no way Amber was letting her out of this job, so she had to find a way to work with Ty Ramsay. Fact two, it wasn't as if he'd ravished her without her consent. She'd been into it just as much as he had been. Playing the maiden wronged was right out. A guy like Ty probably never worried about kissing a woman anyway. He did it all the time, it didn't mean anything. The kind of women he hung out with were sophisticated. They didn't get their worlds rocked by a kiss, likely because they didn't go years between kisses.

Trish squeezed her eyes shut and then opened them again. Okay, numbers worked. First thing, sit at the desk and get back to work. Second thing, act as though it was no big deal. Third thing, she thought, settling down at the table, don't do it again.

It was that pesky third thing that was going to be the problem.

Ty walked back into the room, the phone down by his side. Trish gave him a neutral glance. "All set?" She finished filling out the last form and paper-clipped a cancelled check to it, then checked her watch. "Okay, the checks and autopay forms are filled out, all you need to do is sign them and I'll get them in the mail." She indicated the stack. "I made your appointments and wrote them down on this calendar. The letters just need your signature and they can go. If there's anything else, make a note of it and I'll take care of it tomorrow."

"Trish," he said quietly.

"It's almost five," she continued, ignoring him. "I figured I'd head out unless you needed something else."

"Trish."

"What?" She met his eyes and tried to stifle a more noticeable response.

"Something happened here."

Keep it light and easy, she reminded herself. "Don't sweat it. We were playing around with the script and got carried away. Don't worry about it. It's nothing." She knew how this game was played.

Ty's jaw tightened. "I'm not sure what it was, but I don't think *nothing* is the right word for it."

"Don't go sappy on me, Ty," she said. "I work for you. We'd be better off keeping the physical stuff out of it because it clouds the waters, but I'm not going to go throw myself off a bridge because we kissed."

He walked up, reached out and took her chin in his hand.

"What are you doing?" Trish shook him off in alarm.

"I'm trying to understand something. You were one person at Sabrina's party, you were another one this morning, and now you're someone else. I'm just trying to figure out which one is you."

Trish slung her satchel over her shoulder and walked to the door. "Maybe they all are."

6

SPIDERS HAD the right idea, Trish thought as she walked down the Venice street in the rain. Eight limbs. Too bad she wasn't like them. That way, she calculated, she could have two legs for walking and another three to manage the enormous cardboard portfolios she held and still have a couple to open doors. Like the glass one leading into the Galerie Vizquel.

Propping the cardboard on the wet sidewalk while she worked her way inside wasn't an option. Ty would probably be having kittens if he knew she were even carrying them through the rain, judging by his cautions to her. He must have paid a bundle for the works to be that worried.

Trish sighed.

Heels clicked on the sidewalk behind her. "Here, let me help you." A slender arm reached past her to open the door.

"Thank you so much." Trish turned to see a thin, exquisite-looking woman with a raven-dark asymmetric bob, nearly as tall as Trish in her stylish heels.

"Don't mention it." She waved Trish through, then followed her into the gallery. "The framing area's in the back."

"I take it you work here."

"Live here, more like it." She helped Trish lay the sheets of cardboard on the table. "I'm Jocasta Vizquel, the owner. So what do we have here?"

"Some prints to frame for Ty Ramsay."

Jocasta's mouth curved in pleasure. "I've been waiting for these." She broke the tape and pulled apart the sheets of cardboard. Each held a carefully protected print. Or not prints, exactly, Trish realized, watching Jocasta pull the top tissue away from one.

It might once have started out as a photograph, but the artist had taken it well beyond that. The image was printed on a mosaic of paper squares, a nude woman standing in front of a bed, looking back at the viewer. Color replaced the lines of the photo, giving the gut level impression of sexuality and challenge.

"Nice," Jocasta murmured, setting it aside to look at the next.

"Ty said you'd know what to do with them."

"Oh, I most certainly do." Jocasta laid out another image, this one a landscape. The texture of the paper this time didn't provide counterpoint to the image but rather underscored the lines of what might have been scrub oak and eucalyptus, with a hawk whisking by.

Trish looked at the image and then did a double take. She knew that view, she realized. It was the canyon behind Ty's house. At the bottom of the sheet were the initials *T.R.* The conclusion could only be…

"Ty made these?"

"Of course," Jocasta said. "They're for his show next month."

"But he's an actor," Trish said stupidly.

Jocasta shot her a look. "So?"

Trish stared at the works. She knew Ty could act. Never in a million years would she have suspected he was a talented artist, too. The works held a confidence that spoke of vision and experience. "How long has he been doing this?"

"This?" Jocasta considered while staring at a self-portrait of Ty rendered in tones of sepia. "The textured paper is new. He's been an artist for as long as I've known him. Since college, anyway, or maybe before."

She just couldn't take it in. "I had no idea he was having a show. He never said anything."

"He wouldn't have." Jocasta studied Trish, then glanced back down at the pictures. "Have you known him long?"

Was there a cool tone in her voice or was Trish just imagining it? "I just came on board as his assistant."

Jocasta's eyebrows raised a fraction. "Mr. I'll-never-have-a-staff? Where did he dig you up?"

Trish felt her cheeks heat. "We met at a party."

This time Jocasta's eyes definitely filled with cool dismissal. "Really? And you're working with him." She began measuring the works. "That's our Ty."

"I'm his assistant. That's all I am," Trish emphasized.

"Well, I'm sure you'll be a big help to him." Jocasta glanced up. "I'm all set here. Tell Ty I said hello," she said briskly and turned away, leaving Trish with the distinct feeling she'd been dismissed.

And subtly dissed.

"YOU'RE GOING TO COOK?" Cilla stared at Kelly. "Isn't that what restaurants are for?" Shaking her head, she picked up her drink.

"It's the first time Kev will have seen his parents since we moved in together and it's my first time meeting them, period." Kelly picked up her fork and set it down. "He wants something more, I don't know, intimate than a restaurant."

"This isn't intimate?" Trish asked, raising her voice over the racket that was the L.A. Farmer's Market. The various members of the Supper Club crowded around a couple of plastic tables at Miguel's, tacos and enchiladas before them. Miguel wasn't big on décor and service consisted of an attendant passing laden plastic plates through a slot, but the food was enough to make a person swoon.

Paige watched Kelly toy with a silver twist that hung from her earlobe. "If I didn't know it was impossible, I'd say you were nervous. Take them to a restaurant. It's the perfect location for a family event. Any time anything gets uncomfortable, you can always signal for the waiter." She reached for a taco, taking care to keep the cuff of her goldenrod jacket out of the enchilada sauce.

"They're only here for a few days. I want to get to know them. Anyway, Thea's going to help me plan something foolproof, aren't you, Thea?" Kelly asked.

Thea nodded. "But we've talked about this, Kelly," she said, her voice still raspy from the flu. "It's not going to do you any good unless you do a test run before the big night."

"I will, cross my heart." Kelly marked an X over the

striped Fair Isle sweater she wore. "I really want to do this. I want it to be nice for Kev."

"Ah, young love," Sabrina said with an exaggerated sigh. Kelly stuck out her tongue.

"My vote's with Paige." Delaney reached for another taco. "You can get to know them, just do it in public. That way you get your recon out of the way and you're not a nervous wreck while you do it."

"Don't listen to them, Kelly," Trish said. "Go with your gut. Sometimes you just have to dive in." Of course, that thought only made her think about Ty, which was a mistake.

"Dive in? Like you did at the party last week?" Delaney asked. "One minute you were there and then poof, you were gone."

"You know me and parties." Trish's shrug was casual. So far, she'd managed to avoid questions about just where she'd disappeared to. Lucky for her; if they'd asked, she had no idea what she'd say. Tell Sabrina she'd been gullible enough to get romanced by her cousin at the party? Hardly. Tell her she'd been foolish enough to do it again? No way. Not that it meant anything, of course, but that was a tidbit she'd keep to herself for now. They could laugh about it after. Maybe.

"Well, you missed out," Paige told her. "The documentary was excellent."

"I can't believe I had to miss half of it," Cilla complained. "At least I made it in time for the bondage segment, though. Tie me up, baby. Great stuff."

"I loved that part." Delaney leaned forward with relish. "It's the first thing I've seen on bondage that made it seem like something a normal person would do."

Thea raised her eyebrow. "Any normal person we know?"

"Oh, come on. Don't tell me you haven't at least wondered about it."

Trish remembered the feel of the silk rope around her wrists and shivered.

"I tried it once," Cilla tossed out offhandedly.

"Spill it," Delaney demanded.

"A couple years back. Remember Camera Boy? He took me up to Mendocino one time. We stayed in a room with a four-poster bed."

"You're my idol," Kelly said admiringly. "Hands and feet?"

"Do I do anything by halves?" Cilla grinned. "We raided the robes in the room for their sashes and used his belt and my scarf."

Trish thought of Ty's script, of the scene that called for the heroine to be tied up. What would it be like, she wondered, to live the fantasy, to be well and truly ravished, to give up control completely?

Paige pondered it. "Isn't it a little weird not to be able to move?"

"Sure. The first thing that happens is your nose itches like mad. It goes away, though, as soon as you have something else to think about."

"It always did for me," Sabrina said.

Kelly stared. "You, too?"

"Of course. I needed to connect with my subjects, didn't I?"

"So, about those group-sex segments…" Delaney began.

Sabrina cut her off. "That would be *no*."

"So what's it like, being tied up?" Trish asked.

Cilla grinned. "It's an amazing turn-on. Usually when you're having sex, you're busy doing things and focusing on the other person and all that. Which is wonderful, but when you're tied up, you can't. All you can do is think about how he's going to touch you and where he's going to touch you, and when he finally does, wham!"

"My round was with Bobby the weight lifter," Delaney said dreamily, winding her hair around one finger. "Did that man have a body."

"Scarves?"

"Handcuffs. He had a night job as a security guard," she explained. "He'd hook me to his headboard. We got into the whole role-playing thing—he was a crime boss and my brother owed him money, so I'd be the desperate sister offering myself as his sex slave to do whatever he wanted with me."

"What was your safe word?" Paige asked.

"Daffodil," Delaney said with a bashful smile. "It was what he used to call me. I never had to say it, though. Bobby was a pretty intuitive guy that way. Incredible orgasms. He was dumb as a post about anything beyond sex and weight lifting, but boy, he was good at those two. Perfect justification for meaningless sex," she added as an afterthought before taking a bite of her taco.

"Something to be said for meaningful sex, too," Kelly pointed out.

"No argument here, but sometimes junk-food sex is exactly what I'm in the mood for," Delaney pointed out. "I don't want to deal with anything meaningful. I want it to be something new, something fun and something over."

Trish had always envied Delaney her frank and easy appreciation of men and sex. She acted as though it were of no more consequence than indulging in a dish of ice cream—something to savor, something to appreciate, but when it was gone she was already looking forward to her next dessert.

To Trish, sex was huge, probably because it was such a rare thing in her life. To Delaney, it was good, lighthearted fun. There was something to be said for fun, Trish thought, nibbling on her lip.

"It can be risky," Thea said, as though reading Trish's mind. "It's a good way to wind up in over your head."

"Not if you're prepared for it," Delaney disagreed.

Getting prepared for it was the challenge, of course. Could she, Trish wondered, remembering Ty's mouth.

"We go through different stages." Delaney warmed to her subject, pushing up the sleeves of her denim jacket and flipping her hair out of the way. "I mean, don't get me wrong, I'm all for deep and meaningful sex, but not any time too soon. I think everyone needs to have at least one completely physical affair. How else can you recognize gourmet sex unless you've had fried-pork-rind sex?"

Paige made a face. "Now there's a tasty thought. Thanks for that."

"My pleasure," Delaney laughed.

Trish summoned up an image of Ty and the warnings started churning out of a little slot in her brain. Wrong for her. Dangerous. Heartbreaker. Fatally sincere.

But only if you were expecting something past the moment.

Trish stirred. "Say you've got Mr. Wrong. How do you keep from getting caught up?"

"Know what you want going in." Kelly said decisively. "Sometimes a guy is absolutely perfect in some ways but it's glaringly obvious he won't work in others."

The way it was glaringly obvious that things couldn't possibly work between her and Ty, Trish thought.

"Take Bobby. Physically, we were perfect." She gave a little sigh and then snapped out of it. "In every other way we might as well have been speaking a different language. It was easy to be in bed with him and it was easy for both of us to walk away when we were done." She crunched on a chip. "I knew I didn't want anything more than passing sex from him, so it wasn't a big deal."

Trish considered. Maybe she'd been thinking about it all wrong. She'd been trying to stay the hell away from Ty, but maybe it was her mindset that was wrong. If she knew she didn't want anything more than the moment, what did it matter if he fell out of a crush as quickly as he fell into one? Why should she care if she didn't get anything more than the moment? Hell, she should be happy about it ending, be looking forward to it.

Not, she reminded herself, that she was thinking about the idea in anything more than the abstract. Ty Ramsay was out of her league.

But why did that matter if it was all about the moment, a little niggling voice asked in her head.

"I think that sex is just completely snarled in all these different expectations," Thea spoke up. "It's impossible for anyone to know what they want and expect out of it when every time you turn around, society and the media and your upbringing are all telling you what to think."

"It's probably not for you, Thea," Sabrina suggested.

"It's just hard for me to understand. I know it can work great for some people. I mean, you're comfortable doing it, Delaney, Cilla. You were, Kelly."

"Back in the bad ol' days before she became a bornagain monogamist and moved in with Kev," Cilla said with a wicked wink.

Thea mulled it over. "I don't know, it just seems too easy to make a mistake and wind up confusing sex and love. I'm not sure I could take the chance."

"And Trish wouldn't because she's a hopeless romantic," Delaney added.

No, she never did anything, Trish thought. "I might—you never know," she burst out suddenly. "Maybe it's my turn now." Six heads turned to stare at her. "You guys aren't the only ones who want to have a good time," Trish added defensively.

"Sure," Cilla said, looking a little alarmed, "but it's like they say in those car commercials, 'Professional driver. Don't try this at home.' I don't know if a purely physical affair is the way to go your first time back in the water."

"What better time to do it?" Trish demanded. "I'm not twelve. Besides, I'm sick of always sitting around on the sidelines." She took a breath and told herself to calm down. "Sit back and watch, I might surprise you all."

"That sounds like the voice of a woman with a plan," Sabrina observed. "You have a victim in mind?"

Trish fought the urge to squirm. "Not now, but maybe I'll find one, now that I know what I'm looking for." Think like Delaney, Trish told herself. "Sex doesn't have to be about true love every time you do it, does it?"

"I think you can have sex without bringing all of the overhead into it," Paige agreed. "You just keep it compartmentalized."

"You must keep your guys on a tight leash, Paige, honey," Cilla said. "Are you sure you haven't tried bondage?"

"I'm starting to feel like I'm the only one who hasn't," Kelly complained.

"Well, no one's holding you back."

"Kev and I have been talking about buying a bed," Kelly said thoughtfully. "Maybe we should get one of those four-posters."

"Tell him it's one of the benefits of cohabitating," Delaney contributed.

"One of the many," Kelly said with a wicked smile.

7

BIRDS CHATTERED in the eucalyptus near Ty's house as Trish walked across the parking apron. The morning air felt cool to her, even through her layers. They would have to do, though—she was enough in denial about the approach of winter that she'd refused to wear a jacket. In a concession to vanity, though, she'd ditched her usual sweatshirt for a cotton fisherman's sweater over a dark-green shirt. True, the sweater could have accommodated another person easily and she'd worn it for so many years that the hem sagged to midthigh, but at least she'd made an attempt. Hell, she'd even buttoned her cuffs, as far as that went.

She stood in the shadows at the front door, knocking on the polished wood, anticipation dancing in her stomach. Silly, she told herself. She was just going to work. Her bravado the night before had been one thing, but it wasn't as if she'd been foolish enough to put Ty Ramsay on her hit list. You didn't learn to ski by starting on an Olympic downhill course, at least not if you were smart—and Trish considered herself a very smart woman. No, she'd start with someone easy, maybe Billy the plumber the next time she was working around him. Maybe with someone else.

Except that she couldn't stop thinking about kissing Ty, about the feel of silk wound around her wrists. If a kiss were that good, didn't it follow that the real deal would be incredible?

The idea thrilled and alarmed her. Taking on Delaney's attitude was all well and good, but the problem was that Delaney knew she was good at sex. She'd had lots of practice and more than a few admiring lovers. Trish? She was a little murky on the location and operation of the equipment, even, let alone the technique.

But what about Delaney's idea? If she told herself she didn't want anything long-term, did it really matter if she was embarrassingly inexperienced? After all, if her heart weren't involved, how bad could it be? Think like Delaney, she told herself. Sex was not a life-changing event, not anything that was going to change the course of the world. Just a fun, healthy way to spend time. Trish shivered. The heat of a man's mouth, his bare skin against hers, the sinewy flow of his muscles under her fingers as he slid himself into her. She could think of many apt ways to describe it.

She wasn't sure that fun was remotely adequate.

Trish stirred in the quiet of the morning and knocked again on the door. "Ty? You around?" There was no answer. She hesitated. Come in if he wasn't around, he'd told her. "Ty?" She forced herself to reach out and turn the knob.

As she stepped over the threshold onto the rough marble tiles of the entryway, she faintly heard the sound of the White Stripes singing about falling in love with a girl. She ducked her head outside. No, it was definitely coming from inside the house.

"Hello?" Trish stepped quietly into the entryway, listening to the trickle of the waterfall, and over it the faint strains of music. She had two choices, she supposed. She could sit down and wait until Ty appeared, which meant she'd be wasting a client's time and money, or she could listen to what he'd told her previously and track him down to get started on her day.

But immediately, she felt like a snoop. She was stepping into his private space. That he'd told her to find him didn't help; he wasn't there to lead her personally. The polished wood of the hallway stretched out before her, padded with a central runner covered with a twining pattern in vivid greens and golds. It was the longest hall she'd seen in a house; doors opened off it at intervals, some of them spreading slanting rectangles of sunlight onto the carpet.

Trish had always figured Eve had gotten a bad rap in the Garden of Eden. There was temptation and then there was unbearable temptation. Why blame a person for failing to stand up against the truly impossible? Trish began walking, unable to keep herself from glancing into the open doors to either side as she passed. Okay, so maybe if she'd been a truly virtuous person she'd have just stared forward, but she was this far down the slippery slope already. She might as well indulge herself with another look into the life of Ty Ramsay.

The rooms were enormous. One, with thick, soft carpeting and demure gold walls, appeared to be a guest room. The space held comfort, calm, with a plush fainting couch, fat cushions, and a cozy-looking bed. A red blossom bloomed in a painting on the wall. Georgia O'Keeffe, Trish was pretty sure. Probably an actual Georgia O'Keeffe, considering whose house she was in. Why bother with prints when you could indulge in the real thing?

She looked at the painting more carefully; an odd sexual buzz began deep inside her. There was something about the flower, something that caught and held her attention. Its color held a luminous intensity that pulled her gaze to the center of the image as though she were a honeybee hopelessly drawn. It was just a flower, and yet…

And yet the shadows and folds of the bloom suggested not the petals and stamen of a flower, but the folds and secret hollows of a woman. She couldn't stop staring at the central mystery of the image, the point at which it morphed from innocent floral sexuality to carnal human sensuality.

Trish shook her head and gave a short laugh. Of course. Subliminal suggestion. She'd known that about Georgia O'Keeffe's work. Foolish that it had taken her by surprise now.

Foolish to feel this undercurrent of arousal and excitement.

The next room drew a soft "Oh" from her. It didn't offer excitement, but something much more necessary—comfort. It was a library, complete with coffered ceiling and emerald-green walls lined with bookshelves. Trish couldn't resist taking a step inside, her feet sinking into the thick Turkish carpet. She'd never have guessed that Ty read so much, but then she'd never have picked him as an artist. It was the second time she'd bumped her nose on her preconceived notions of him and she was a bit chagrined.

But she was even more intrigued.

The volumes that filled the shelves weren't the kind of stamped leather editions that people bought by the caseload to dress their walls. They were mostly battered-looking paperbacks, some hardbounds, all a little worse for the wear in a way that suggested they were old and treasured friends. If she'd been told to guess what type of books he read, she'd have guessed legal thrillers and the like. Certainly, some of those were in evidence, but at a glance there were also some sublime literary novels, dark comedies, science fiction, even a couple of nonfiction. She recognized a few of her favorites and others that were on her mental to-be-read list.

It was nothing she expected, but she was beginning to discover that Ty Ramsay defied expectation. She itched to continue looking. Studying what a person read was tantamount to looking into his soul. Still…

She glanced at her watch and withdrew hastily. Perhaps another time she could go through his books at leisure, with his permission. For now, she had work to do.

She passed a workout room with rubberized floor, walls of mirrors, and a collection of free weights. No Nautilus machines for him, it appeared. Judging by the way his back and shoulders had felt, though, he made good use of his equipment. Her palms tingled with the memory of touching him. What would it be like, she wondered. Did it really not matter if he was totally unsuitable in every way but the physical? Perhaps, going by Delaney, that was all the more reason to imagine being hot, wet, and naked against him. Trish brushed her fingertips down her neck and shivered a bit. Work, she reminded herself, she was here to work, not fantasize about the client, no matter how delectable he might be.

As Trish neared the sun-drenched end of the hall, the music grew louder. Ty had to be down there, somewhere, in the room with all the light and she was going to find him. Trish gave a glance in the final open door as she passed and stopped dead.

It was his bedroom.

And what a bedroom. The walls were a sapphireblue color, completely rich and decadent-looking. In fact, the whole room vibrated with a sense of indulgence. Let the rest of the house be stylishly low-key and minimalist. In this room, Ty had gone beyond his sense of design to indulge himself with color, texture, luxury. A dark, polished bureau sat against one wall, holding a bronze lamp and a mahogany chest. The lines of a nearby highboy were sleek, the wood different enough to keep it from blending in, similar enough to please the eye. And the bed…

The bed was massive and high, with thick, elaborately carved posts at each corner. It made her think of a king's chamber. The duvet and pillows provided a feast of color: wine, gold, emerald green, deep blue, tossed together in a randomness more appealing than order. She'd never seen a bed so high, so wildly divine. It would hit just about at the tops of her thighs, she calculated.

And it had four posts, her mind shouted. The kind of bed a person could be tied up in, sinking back in all that comfort, feeling the bonds that promised pleasure. *All you can do is think about how he's going to touch you and where he's going to touch you.* Her hands, pulled up over her head, her breasts, bare to his hands.

Ravished.

On the wall was an abstract that managed somehow to suggest two forms twined together. Rust and ocher, brick and dark gold, the colors twisted and flowed. Perhaps it was the sense of movement that started arousal tugging deep in her belly, the palpable sense of desire trapped within the frame. It was two lovers wrapped in urgency, consumed in a dance of ecstasy. Two lovers with no thought of anything but one another.

And pleasure.

"Do you like abstracts?"

Trish turned to find Ty standing at the end of the hallway, staring at her, the sunlight from the open door behind him gilding his hair. She didn't jump because it was somehow right that he was there. "I don't know, is it an abstract?" she asked as he walked toward her. Perhaps she should have been embarrassed to be caught staring into his bedroom. She couldn't make herself care. What thrummed through her as she locked eyes with him was wanting, pure and simple.

Ty stopped dead, his eyes darkening. For a humming instant, neither of them moved. Then he stepped forward to catch her hand and lead her inside. Into the room.

The heat from his fingers bloomed throughout her body. The curve of his mouth mesmerized her as he spoke. "It's just color, not form. Look." He led her up to it.

Her fingers itched to stroke the carved edges of his cheekbones; instead, she reached out to touch the frame of the painting. "I don't see abstract color."

"What do you see?"

She turned to him. "Lovers. They're completely caught up in each other." She indicated the lines, remembering a hot kiss in the moonlight, the feel of Ty's arms around her. "You can see them holding each other, kissing. The wanting takes your breath away. Can't you feel it?" She turned to Ty to find him only inches away, focused on her, not the painting.

And the words dried up in her throat.

As if mesmerized, Ty reached out to trace his fingertips down her cheek, so lightly that she could barely feel the contact. Arousal vaulted through her.

He leaned near. It was as though she were watching a scene in a movie, maybe because she'd watched him so many times shifting closer to the camera, closer to the woman he wanted. But this wasn't a movie. It wasn't in front of her on a fifty-foot screen, it was happening to her, for real, here and now.

And then his mouth was on hers.

It was as though she'd been transported into the painting, desire twisting around her thick and unyielding. She yearned and she tasted the hot pleasure of his mouth. She longed and she felt his arms wrapped around her, pressing her to him. She wanted and she felt him tighten against her.

And after all of the years of isolation, it was as though some part of her was bursting free. How long had she been the Trish who didn't touch people? The Trish who was alone? The Trish who was afraid to let herself want? Now, wanting was wound into the fiber of her being, it shimmered around her.

Ty kissed her lips, her cheeks, her neck, half caressing, half devouring. She could feel the urgency vibrating through him, whispering in the touch of his hands as they slid up under her sweater to search out the curves of her breasts. Underneath her shirt, he discovered the startling secret that her breasts were bare.

Trish chuckled down in her throat when she heard him let out an explosive breath even as he ran his fingers over the hard point of her nipple. "You planned this to drive me crazy, right?" he asked raggedly, then slid his other hand up to the nape of her neck.

"You need to tell me if this is not going to happen." His voice was rough with wanting. When she said nothing, he took them both deep with a kiss that made everything recede except the intoxicating heat, and the urgent need to find more.

Eve, Trish thought, filled with the urge to feel him naked against her. There truly was such a thing as more temptation than a person could bear. And at that point, you forgot about what was smart and what was sensible and took, just took. She could be like the rest of them, she could have sex for its own sake. Why not open herself up to pleasure and say to hell with what came after? Who cared if nothing was going to come after, so long as she could wallow in this mindbending moment first?

"It's going to happen," she murmured, as much to herself as to him. "Everything's going to happen."

THEY WERE STILL STANDING, she realized, sunlight glowing through the shades, slanting through the doorway. Ty pulled her shirt loose from her jeans and slipped his hand beneath the cloth. Her quiet moan was in perfect time with Ty's groan as his fingers slid over her skin.

"You're so soft," he chanted again and again, running his hand up the flat of her stomach, lingering over the curve of her waist, and filling his hand with the weight of her full breast.

Arousal thrummed within her. When he rolled her nipple between his fingers, she cried out at the intensity, cried out against his mouth.

Suddenly, she was desperate to have him against her. She reached out to tug his T-shirt loose and pull it off over his head. His body took her breath away, all taut muscle and smooth power. Clothing gave him a deceptive leanness, she realized, slipping out of her shoes as she ran her hands over his shoulders. His abs shuddered under her fingers as she traced the lines of muscle and the thin trail of hair that formed at his navel and led down to his waistband.

No nerves, Trish ordered herself, and unbuttoned his jeans.

With a growl, Ty reached down to pick her up.

"Put me down," she said in sudden alarm. "I'm too heavy."

"I'll put you down all right," he said, lifting her with ease and laying her on the bed. Her jeans were unzipped and gone before she could react. He dragged her sweater and shirt over her head. The buttoned cuffs caught on her hands, though, and Ty made a noise of frustration. "Leave it," Trish whispered, smothering the shyness with the thrill that vaulted through her. "I want you against me, now."

He stood back to strip off his jeans and toss them aside, and then he was on the bed with her, all startling warmth and hardness against her. Trish gave a gasping laugh. "That feels amazing," she managed.

"You think that's amazing, just wait."

Every touch, every brush, tantalized, the slick promise of his tongue tracing over her collarbones, the slide of his hand over the curve of her hip. And then his mouth and hand met at the soft swell of her breast and her body bucked against him. "Careful," Ty murmured, setting his hand over her wrists to pin them in place. Suction, liquid warmth, the scrape of teeth against her excruciatingly sensitive flesh—the arousing constraint made her focus on sensation and sensation alone. Trish could feel the hot coil of tension tightening down low, down where she was still crying out to be touched.

Ty shifted to her other breast, lingering until she was moaning. Her body arched like a bow against his mouth. He raised his head to look at her, his eyes dark with passion. She was making love, she, Trish. She was naked with a man and he wanted her. Letting go of her wrists, he licked his way down her belly, then lower still. He put his mouth on her, inhaling her secret scent, and she cried out.

Next time I'll make him stretch it out, but not this time, she thought feverishly. This time she had no patience for finesse. Freeing her wrists in a frenzied scattering of buttons and tearing cloth, she clutched at his shoulders as if to increase the slick, soft friction. He moved one hand up to her breast, rolling the nipple between his fingers, and still he drove her with lips and tongue. Any whisper of shyness was over. She couldn't stop moving her hips, moaning out her pleasure at each new touch.

When he pushed a finger inside her, pleasure fired out to every nerve in her body. Dimly, she heard herself crying out, felt her hips bucking, and still it continued tightening in intensity until she felt she couldn't bear any more. Finally, it faded enough so that she could breathe.

Ty moved up the bed to fasten his mouth over hers, and that quick, demanding arousal returned. But it wasn't about her, now, it was about him. She knew what to do. She'd heard the stories, she'd read the books. Now all that remained was to do it.

Trish searched for courage and dropped her hand down to find him hard and pulsing. Her touch tore a ragged sound out of him and she felt an immediate thrill. She could arouse him. She could make him lose control. Reaching between her thighs, she found slickness and spread it over the head of his erection. Then she returned to stroking him up and down, noticing when he quivered, when he groaned.

Ty's breath hissed in and he kissed her, hard. Then he hooked his fingers in the sides of her underwear and dragged them down her legs. Trish felt a surge of adrenaline as he positioned himself between her thighs. Her breath caught in her chest. This was it, what she'd wondered about, what she'd wanted. Finally, she was going to feel it the way it was really supposed to be.

Ty looked down at her, his eyes almost luminous in their color. She heard a crackle of foil. A moment later something smooth and hard and warm rubbed against her clitoris, making her gasp, then traced the cleft below it. And then, with a push of his hips, he slid in to fill her.

She let go with the shock and the pleasure and the glory of it all. She'd never known this: this urgent heat, this driving hardness, this jolting sensation. It hadn't been this way with Brett—her only memory was of hard hipbones and the pain of him pushing himself in when she was still too dry. There was none of this amazing surge that left her reeling, that drove her to wrap her legs around Ty's waist and grab him and tell him now. *Now.*

And then she was shuddering, gasping, arching even as Ty groaned and spilled himself into her.

8

TRISH STOOD in the shower under pounding hot water. Big enough to hold a small bed, the stall from chest down was faced in slate. A sheet of glass block formed the upper portion, bringing in a flood of daylight and an impression of greenness from the landscape outside.

Now, the daylight consisted of afternoon shadows. They'd spent half the day making love, she thought bemusedly, rinsing her hair. It had been like nothing she'd ever been through before. Not the quick, clumsy, painful interludes she'd known. Perfectly executed? No, but being able to fall back laughing with Ty defused any awkwardness she might have felt.

At last they'd worn each other out, and it was clear that they had to move on. It was then that Trish had gotten the attack of nerves. She'd been so focused on the sex part—with good reason—that she'd never found out how a person managed to actually come to a casual sex understanding. Delaney made it sound as if it was pretty much an underlying assumption. Was that the way to handle it? She made a mental note to ask Delaney next time the subject came up, and turned off the water.

The shower had been her escape. Ty hadn't, as she'd feared he would, offered to join her, perhaps wanting space of his own, perhaps understanding her own need for it. Instead, he'd gotten her an absurdly plush, emerald-green bath sheet, kissed her and left.

Trish felt a smile spread over her face as she pulled the towel from its heated rack. Okay, so the kissing and leaving part had been rather time-consuming and complicated. Somewhere around the climax of the most delicious of the complications, she had been tempted to pull him into the stall with her, but realized she needed the time to regroup. A *long* time later, he finally had left.

Now, she stood in front of the mirror, drying herself. She rubbed a finger over the dark smudge of a bruise on her thigh and gave a fatuous smile. He'd wanted her so badly he'd lost his customary control. Butterflies skittered in her stomach as she remembered the feel of his body atop hers, the feel of his cock inside her. Now she knew what it was all about, finally, finally and it was *wonderful*. She wanted to shout with elation.

However psyched she was, though, she still had to be practical. It was just sex. It didn't mean anything. It couldn't. As far as Ty was concerned, Trish was sure she was just a novelty and one he was bound to tire of. Her mind shied away from that part. She'd be okay with it, she reminded herself as she slid into her panties and jeans. If Delaney and Cilla and Kelly could do it, she could do it, too. She picked up her shirt and looked at the torn cuffs. A smile tugged at the corners of her mouth. Sweater only, it looked like. She'd keep the shirt as her badge of honor.

Ty wasn't anywhere to be seen when Trish came out, hair still a little damp. In the hallway, she noted that the music had changed to Evanescence. She let it lead her to him. Down the hallway, Trish paused at the open door and caught a breath of pure pleasure.

Golden light streamed into the room—or rather, the studio. The two white inside walls soared twelve feet or more to the ceiling. Glass formed the two outside walls, rising and curving over to form an atrium of sorts so that the border between indoors and outdoors faded into nothingness. It felt as though the canyon had come inside.

It wasn't a vanity studio. Canvases filled a series of built-in vertical storage slots; others leaned up against the walls or sat on easels. A rack of table-mounted pigeonholes held brushes, paint, palette knives and other things she couldn't identify. On one wall, drying photographic prints hung from a line next to a door that presumably led to a darkroom.

And in the center, at a table, sat Ty. Paintbrush in hand, he studied the work before him. Slashes of color across the canvas proved, when she stared at them, to be a view of a man's face, though not Ty's.

For a moment, she just stared, amazed afresh at the reality of him. That someone like him was in her life, however briefly, was stupefying. Seconds passed as she watched silently, not wanting to disturb him as he stared at the paper and added another bit of shading. His expression was intent, the motion of his hands confident.

The way they'd been confident touching her.

Ty set his brush down then and glanced over at her.

His face lit up with genuine pleasure. He rose and crossed to her. "Hey, you," he said, sliding one hand around the nape of her neck and pulling her close to linger over her mouth until she felt herself melting.

Those lips, those eyes. Lethal. Absolutely lethal, Trish thought, when the silliness went away. "So." She surveyed the studio. "The Secret Life of Ty Ramsay?"

His grin was quick and crooked. "Not secret," he disagreed moving back over to his worktable. "Just low-key."

"Very low-key. I guess the prints you had me take in for framing were yours, huh?" Trish followed him.

Even in a paint-spattered shirt, with his hair spiky and disordered from being in bed, he had a presence about him, something larger than life. Then he smiled at her, his eyes crinkling, and she relaxed. It wasn't someone larger than life, it was Ty, and everything was going to be okay.

"What did you think of them?" he asked, his voice a bit too casual as he added a final dash of color to his canvas.

"I was impressed." And touched by the fact that he was just a little uncertain about his art. "They stuck with me. They made me want to see them again. So why don't you talk to the press about it? I've never read anything."

He scrubbed a hand through his hair, leaving a paint streak that made him look like an '80s punker. "It's not like it's a state secret or anything. I just don't talk about it a lot."

It puzzled her. "Why not? You must know you've got

talent." She leaned her elbows on the table, her face level with his.

"It's a little like saying you're a mime or something, isn't it?" Ty said in amusement. "As far as most people are concerned, I'm an actor. That's the slot they want to put me in. Like I said, I just keep it low-key."

"Well, there's low-key and there's low-key. The desert image hanging in your living room is yours, isn't it? You didn't even sign it."

She'd been seduced by his charm, enthralled by his looks. She never expected to find his bashful grin endearing.

"I knew when I finished it that I was going to want to have it out where I could see it. It's not like I'm going to forget who did it."

"But with your talent and your visibility, you could be hugely successful."

Ty reached out to brush his fingertips against the ends of her hair, already curling in the dry California air. "So your hair is really curly, huh? How did you get it so straight the night we met?"

"Cilla has magical powers. Don't think you're changing the subject, though."

"Oh, no?" He stroked his knuckles against her cheek.

Trish straightened up hastily. Letting him touch her would change the subject really quickly. "No. Answer the question."

Shaking his head, Ty carried his dirty brushes over to the sink and began to wash them. "I don't know. I'm not exactly in need of money, so what's the point? To have a big crush at the opening? Don't need it.

And I don't want to do inferior work and have it sell out just because it's me. That'd make me an opportunistic hack."

"But you know it's not inferior work," Trish protested, following him. "That's not just me talking. Jocasta thinks so, too, and you've gotten some good reviews."

Ty flicked her a sardonic glance. "Trust me, after eight years in film, I've learned exactly how relative the worth of a review can be," he said, pressing a brush dry with a soft cloth before reaching for the next one.

"So, HAVE YOU DONE a show before?"

"Jocasta's hung some of my work in the past, but just as a side thing. I haven't trotted myself out for the circus before."

"Circus, hmm?" Trish leaned one hip against the counter. "So why show your art now, since you obviously don't believe in it?"

To let it breathe? Ty began to wash the last brush, the silky bristles between his fingers reminding him of the feel of Trish's skin. "Art shut up in a studio isn't alive. It needs to be seen. Besides, Jocasta and I go way back. Her gallery could use the boost."

"It's a chance to introduce what you're doing to the broader art community," Trish pointed out. "That doesn't seem like such a bad thing."

"I suppose."

"You don't sound all that convinced. Are you worried about how they'll take it? You shouldn't be, you know your work is solid. Besides, this should be famil-

iar territory for you. You put yourself out there every
time you do a film."

"Not the same. It's…"

"More personal?"

"Maybe." Ty kept his eyes on her. She'd dressed with
little apparent vanity, shoving the sleeves of her sweater
up to her elbows, leaving her hair a damp tumble of curls.
How was it she was more enticing to him than ever?

"What drives you to it?"

A good question that deserved a good answer,
though he wasn't sure how to explain the compulsion
to create. "I don't know," he said finally. "I just have
to. When you work on a film, it's dozens of people
teaming up, all wanting to stamp their little piece of it
with their vision. I need something that's just me. I see
these images and I need to make them real." He shook
his head. "Does that make sense?"

"Yes." Trish gave him a thoughtful look. "It's a part
of you and you want to protect it."

"It's not that." He struggled to clarify it. "I just want
it to be given a fair shake."

"You mean you want to be taken seriously."

They were the words he'd resisted saying because he
knew just how fatuous they would sound. "It sounds
like such a cliché."

"No it doesn't. You've got every right to feel that,"
she insisted. "People should judge you on what you do,
not who you are."

If only it were that easy. "Rights don't really come
into it when the media is concerned. I'm an action hero.
Why should they give me the time of day as an artist?"

Trish fixed him with her gaze. "It doesn't matter what they do or don't want to do. They won't have a choice. Your art is real, Ty. People are going to see that."

"Sometimes I think I'd be smarter just to leave things as they are, forget about the opening."

"You don't strike me as the type to let anyone intimidate you into giving up something important."

He studied the glow of her skin in the afternoon light. Not just a pretty face, this one, he thought. And it meant something—a lot—that she'd take up for him. "All right," he said, in reluctant amusement, "maybe you've got a point."

Trish's lips quirked. "They'll take you seriously, sooner or later. And you'll enjoy the opening."

"I might if it weren't going to be a mob scene." That was always the rub. His life was open season, no matter how private he wanted things to be. "If I thought it could just be a normal opening."

"Define normal opening. I'm sure Warhol openings were mob scenes, too. Forget the whole celebrity thing," she said impatiently. "Trust Jocasta to take care of it and look at this as a chance to network with a whole different community."

The question was, would the community see it that way or would they hammer him because he'd had the temerity to try to cross fields? "I just don't want to have reviewers or collectors mix up one thing for the other."

"You're nervous."

"And you notice way too much," he said lightly. "I

don't know if *nervous* is the right word. This is something that's been a part of me for a long time. Since way before I got into acting." He dried his hands and tossed the towel into a hamper, then leaned over to kiss her and lost long minutes to the spicy sweet taste of her.

"All right, already," he said finally, straightening. "Enough of talking about my art. We've got more important things to settle here. Let's go out in the living room. We need to talk."

"About what?" The alarm that flitted over her face made him wonder. There were riddles here he'd yet to solve.

"Scriptwriting."

"Oh, that." Her shoulders relaxed perceptibly. "Well, let's go then," she said briskly.

WARNING HERSELF not to expect anything, Trish sat cautiously at one end of the couch. Ty grabbed a copy of the script and flopped down next to her, kicking his feet up on the coffee table.

"I took your script changes in to the rehearsal yesterday," he said, flipping through the pages.

"How did that go?" She wished he hadn't distracted her by sitting so close. She wanted, *oh, she wanted,* to touch him, but she didn't know if that was part of the understanding they had. She didn't know if they even *had* an understanding. Maybe their understanding was no understanding, just sex if and when they happened to fall into bed together. She glanced up and saw him watching her with an odd smile on his face. "What?"

"Did you hear anything I just said?" he asked.

"About the script? Um, no."

He grinned and stretched his arm out along the back of the couch to toy with her hair. "Everybody liked your script changes."

Trish gave him a doubtful look. "Everybody?"

"The director, the other cast members. And I did, of course, although admittedly I might be a little biased."

"What about the scriptwriter?"

"He wasn't thrilled at first," Ty admitted. "He agreed that the revisions worked, though. He didn't have a whole lot of choice. Anyway, he's on deadline on another project and probably happy to be shut out of problems with this one." Idly, he stroked the back of one finger along her jawline.

Focus on the discussion, Trish reminded herself. "You told them the changes were from you, I hope."

"I don't take credit for other people's work," he told her. "You wrote it and that's what I told them." The corners of his mouth, that delectable mouth, tugged up into a grin. "At least once they'd said they liked them. The director's fine with it. A screen credit's a long shot, but you might get a guild card out of it."

Ruthlessly, she suppressed the little surge of excitement—it was a long way from idle conversation to guild cards. "So does the screenwriter hate me for messing with his baby?"

Ty shook his head. "I told you, this kind of thing happens all the time. You don't last long in this business if you have a fragile ego. So will you do it? Will you keep working on the script with me?"

Trish thought of the hour she'd spent the night before working on her own screenplay, feeling the personalities flowing out on the page as she bore witness to the gradual blossoming of Callie, and the tightening of the vise around Michael. How would she feel if some outsider with no knowledge of who they were came in and ran roughshod over characters she cared about? "I don't know, Ty. It feels sort of heartless."

"Even if it winds up being a better movie? He'll get the major credit, even if we rewrite it for him. You're not taking away his glory—or his paycheck. You're just helping all of us make it better."

"You're sure?"

"I'm positive. Trust me."

She studied him. "All right."

"So what about working on a script of your own, as good as you are?"

Trish just smiled and made a noncommittal noise. "Right now, let's work on the script we've got."

He took her hand between his and kissed her fingertips. His lips were soft against them. "All right, where should we start?"

"How about the spanking scene?" she asked, mischief glinting in her eyes.

Ty blinked. "I don't remember a spanking scene."

"You know, the one where the hero gets tied up and the heroine paddles him?" Trish laughed at him.

With a mock frown, Ty shifted her on the couch so that she was lying back and leaned over her. "Oh, we need to cut that scene. I think we should sub in another one with the hero and heroine making love." He brushed his lips over hers.

"We don't want to bore the audience with too much of a good thing," Trish managed, even as she felt herself slipping away into that haze of desire.

"Trust me," he murmured against her lips, "you can never have too much of a good thing."

9

"You *WHAT?*"

Trish's laugh echoed in the health-club locker room. "I had sex." She pulled her stretchy blue workout shirt over her head.

"When?" Cilla stood in front of her locker, staring down at her.

"Yesterday. And today."

"Yesterday night?"

"No, morning." A smile tugged at the corners of her mouth. "Actually, pretty much all day, now that I think about it. He obviously takes his vitamins."

"I thought you had a glow to you." Cilla leaned down and hugged her. "Oh my God, tell me everything. Where did you meet him? How did it all happen so fast?"

How, indeed? Trish wondered. It felt so improbable that it was as though it was happening to someone else, and at the same time she'd been bursting to tell Cilla. *I'm different. I'm a grown-up. I finally understand.* "I don't know. It's been a wild ride."

"You look fabulous. Now tell me all about him."

Trish's heart sank. "There's not much to tell." She

should have expected that Cilla would want to share in the details of her triumph. It was what they'd always done, not that Trish had ever had much to add. Normally, of course, it would have been a blast to relive every minute in detail. But given who she'd done the living with…

Cilla draped her jacket over the hanger that held her transparent turquoise-and-black Marc Jacobs dress. "Little Trish, doing the wild thing all day." She paused a moment as she slipped out of the foundation garment and zipped it into her garment bag. "Wait a minute, now let me catch up here. How can you be having sex all day? I thought you said earlier you had a new client. Are you playing hooky from Amber?" She pulled on her yoga shorts and then stopped as the light dawned. "Wait a minute, is the love god your *client?*"

Trish couldn't suppress the grin. "Well, it's sure not the plumber."

"Does Amber know? Never mind," she said before Trish could open her mouth. "Dumb question. Forget I asked. So come on, details."

"There's not that much to tell."

Cilla snorted. "You go to bed with a man after, what, five years, and you say there's not much to tell?"

"There isn't," Trish said awkwardly, grabbing her mat and rising from the bench in front of the lockers. "Anyway, class is going to start in a couple of minutes. We should get into the other room."

"Oh, right, I'm supposed to concentrate on my poses after that bombshell?" Cilla followed her through the door into the asana room.

Bamboo matting covered the walls; the floor was polished hardwood. In a corner, candles flickered on a carved wood table, scenting the air with vanilla. The effect was one of quiet serenity. A soft duet of flute and harp played over the stereo. At the front of the room, the yoga instructor sat quietly in the lotus position with her eyes closed.

Trish walked to an empty patch toward the back of the room and laid out her mat.

Cilla dropped down beside her. "At least tell me your new boy's name."

Trish sat with her legs outstretched before her, raised her hands high over her head, and took a deep breath. "He's not my new boy. He's just someone I'm having sex with."

"Run that by me again?"

"Someone I'm having sex with. Casual sex." She bent from the waist, exhaling and stretching out over her toes. "You and Delaney don't have a lock on it, you know."

"Hey, I've seen your version of the downward dog. I'm sure you can do anything you want to." Cilla lay on her back and brought her knees up to her chest, wrapping her arms around them. "Physically, anyway. Emotionally, though? You're a hopeless romantic, Trish. You are not built to just screw around. Are you sure you know what you're doing?"

"I'm sick of waiting around for Mr. Right." Trish straightened, stretching her fingers toward the ceiling and bent again. "I wanted to have sex while I'm still young enough to do it."

"Oh, ancient you."

Trish made a face at her.

Cilla laughed, then sobered. "I just don't want to see you get hurt."

"I'm alive. Being hurt kind of goes with the process, doesn't it? Anyway, it's unlikely in this case," she said briskly. "I'm going into it with my eyes open." She was, wasn't she?

Cilla studied her and then gave a slow grin. "I guess I should have given you a makeover a long time ago. Want me to help you pick out some work clothes?"

"He doesn't seem to care what kind of clothes I wear," Trish gave a little laugh, realizing as she said it that it was true.

"Maybe he just wants you out of them." Cilla stretched over to touch her toes. "So what's his name?"

Trish hesitated.

The yoga instructor at the front of the room stirred. "Okay, everyone, let's sit up straight, legs crossed, lotus position if you can manage it."

"Come on," Cilla whispered. "Throw me a bone. What do you call him besides boss?"

It was her own fault for being so excited she had to tell her best friend, Trish thought. "Ty."

"Ty," Cilla repeated, trying for the lotus and settling for tucking one leg against the other. "Very sexy," she said approvingly. "And is Ty—" she stopped. "Ty who?"

"Um, Ty Ramsay," Trish said, wondering why her voice was suddenly so high.

"You're having sex with Sabrina's cousin?" Cilla stared in amazement.

Heads turned.

"Can you say that a little louder?" Trish hissed. She laid her hands on her knees and took a deep breath, and looked for serenity. "Breathe."

"Believe me," Cilla assured her, "I'm trying."

"OKAY," CILLA SAID as they filed back into the locker room. "You want to try meaningless sex, I'm totally behind you. But Ty Ramsay? Isn't it a little like learning to walk on the interstate?"

Trish shrugged as she dialed the combination on her lock. "Delaney said pick someone totally unsuitable. Well, that would be him."

"No argument there." Cilla pulled out her garment bag and slung it over her arm. "I'm just trying to figure out the why. Outside of the obvious, I mean," she added.

"Simple. I know from the git go that nothing can happen because it never does with him." And she wasn't going to expect anything, she reminded herself.

"But you've listened to Sabrina. He's going to break your heart, honey. That's what he does."

"It's not him, it's what the other women expect from him." Trish slung her workout bag over her shoulder.

"Oh God, you're defending him already."

"I'm not. It just doesn't apply to me. The ones who get their hearts broken are the ones who go looking for more than sex," Trish insisted. "Me, I just want to fool around. I'm channeling Delaney."

"I wouldn't even trust Delaney with Mr. Sincere," Cilla objected as they finished changing, grabbed their gear and walked out into the lobby.

"Well, it's a good thing she isn't sleeping with him, then, isn't it?" The night air felt cool against Trish's heated cheeks as they walked to the parking lot.

"Look, this conversation is *so* not over," Cilla said. "We're going to dinner and you're going to tell me what happened."

"Only if you promise not to lecture me."

"I won't lecture you. I don't guarantee I won't have anything else to say on the topic of Mr. Ramsay, but I'm also dying of curiosity. Tell me!"

"Well, remember when you left me at the party?" Trish began.

THEY SAT AT A CORNER TABLE in Louise's Bistro, the remains of their dinner scattered around them. Cilla took a sip of her wine and looked over the table. "So what is it about us that we can't talk about our lives without food and alcohol present?"

"It does take a lot out of you," Trish agreed.

"It's an energetic topic. Especially people like you. I'll never look at a shower massage the same way again."

"Cleanliness is next to godliness."

Cilla grinned and dipped a bit of bread in olive oil. "In the interest of avoiding heresy, I'm just going to leave that one alone."

"Smart move." Trish smiled.

Cilla cleared her throat. "So wasn't I a good listener?"

"You were a great listener."

"Do I get points for refraining from lecturing?"

"Why do I have a bad feeling about this?"

Cilla grinned. "Hear me out. I'm just thinking that the last time I heard someone insisting they'd be fine with just sex and they weren't going to get involved, it was Sabrina. You're sounding an awful lot like her."

"Totally different situation," Trish objected. "They'd had a mad pash before. We always knew she was in love with him. She was the only one who hadn't figured it out."

"My point, exactly. Actually, the point is, she was in over her head from the beginning."

"But she's happy now."

Cilla stared at her, eyes troubled. "Trish, I know I'm being tough on you here, but please tell me you're not hoping for happily ever after with Ty Ramsay."

"I'm not looking for anything from Ty but a good time." She couldn't possibly afford to think of anything else, Trish reminded herself. Those were the ground rules.

"Well, all right." Cilla cleared her throat. "While we're talking about tough love, you know there's a whole 'nother issue out there you haven't even touched on."

"Telling Sabrina." Trish closed her eyes. "She's going to think I'm crazy."

"Likely," Cilla agreed.

"But I can't not tell her, that's the thing that's driving me crazy."

"Assuming you're not already there."

"Assuming. I mean, it's common courtesy, I know that. Then again, given that it's just a casual affair, do I really have to bother her? I mean, what would you do?"

"You're the only one who can make that call," Cilla said.

"What would you want if you were Sabrina?"

"Let's turn the tables. What would *you* want?"

Trish massaged her temples to ward off the sudden headache. "It's so hard to figure. I mean, I think I'd want to know. Oh, who am I kidding," she said impatiently. "Of course I'd want to know. I need to tell her, but God, I dread it."

"In that case, I've got a piece of good news for you. I talked with Kelly today and she says Sabrina and Stef leave tomorrow for Greece, to work on his documentary."

"I thought they were done shooting."

"Guess you never have enough footage," Cilla said lightly. "So anyway, you're off the hook on telling Sabrina, at least for the short term."

And in the long term, Trish thought, things with Ty would be over. And she was fine with that, just fine.

Really.

10

Ty STARED INTENTLY into her eyes. "Which is the real you—" he asked "—glossy and sexy or brisk and efficient? Who do you want to be?"

"It's not up to me," she responded in a faltering voice. "It doesn't matter which one is me, I have to do my job."

"The reality is," Ty said silkily "they're both you."

"There is no me and…and hellfire, ladies and gentlemen, I just said the wrong line." The actress, Caitlyn Reynolds, broke off her probing gaze into Ty's face and flushed. "Sorry, guys." She'd made a name for herself in the lead role of a television spy series. Now, two years later she was embarking on her first film role and she was palpably nervous, even though it was only rehearsal. Ty took pains to put her at her ease, Trish noticed, with jokes and gentle teasing.

But it was Trish that he looked to, and to Trish that he flashed the quick smile of promise.

She wasn't quite sure how she'd wound up here, sitting in a thirty-eighth-floor conference room in the offices of Velocity Productions, watching the cast of *Dark Touch* running scenes. Then again, she wasn't quite sure how it was that she'd found herself in the midst of a full-blown affair with Ty Ramsay. It was as though she were inhabiting someone else's life. Perhaps the life of her alter ego, a life of excitement, arousal and sex, she thought, feeling a little shiver as she watched Ty across the room.

But it wasn't someone else's life, and she wasn't a different person. Not really. She dressed the same, she looked the same, she did the same job during the day. And if she started the days off with hot and urgent sex and spent her nights in Ty's bed, it was purely a fluke, wasn't it?

She had to remember that, she had to remind herself it was nothing more. The time they had together was limited, no matter how she looked at it. If nothing else, Ty's infatuation would eventually wear off as it always did. More to the point, principal photography began in two weeks. Interiors first, he'd told her, which meant they'd do all of the scenes in the S&M club, not to mention the bondage scenes with Caitlyn.

And Ty Ramsay always fell for his costars.

"Okay people," said Dale Westhoff, the director, "it might not be immortal but let's work with it."

Ty and Caitlyn faced each other in their chairs. Trish watched them together as they built an artificial world and made it real. And her mind focused on ways to make the script work.

"If you're there, you can watch us and write down your ideas," Ty had said that morning. "You're my assistant. Nobody's going to think anything of you being in the room."

"Wanna bet?"

He'd looked at her with a glint of mischief in his eyes. "Sure."

"It was a figure of speech," she'd said impatiently. "My point is that it's not feasible for some inexperienced outsider to give input on a script."

"It is if the input's good, and I've already told you Dale liked the last rewrites."

"They'll never tolerate it."

"Oh, I think they will, and I'm so sure of it I'm willing to make a little wager on it. How about this? We go to the rehearsal and just walk in. If anyone says anything about you being in the room, you win."

She'd raised an eyebrow. "Since I'm almost sure to win, what do I get?"

Ty had thought a moment. "You win, I'm your slave for the entire weekend."

"And if they don't say anything?"

"If they don't say anything, I win and you're my slave for the entire weekend."

In the end, she'd agreed. But what had seemed reasonable at the time had become more improbable by the moment as they'd crossed Velocity's bright lobby, a space lined with framed movie posters and graced by a life-sized cardboard cutout of Ty as the hero of *Demolition*. Half the people in L.A. fancied themselves amateur screenwriters. That didn't mean that any director worth his salt would let one of them sit in on a rehearsal, no matter how much Ty insisted they would. Ty didn't know what he was talking about, she'd sniffed.

He had, of course, and she should have known it.

When they'd arrived in the conference room, the director, assistant directors and half dozen cast members hadn't looked twice at her.

"Why should they care?" Ty had shown her to a seat and handed her a copy of the screenplay. "We've got a script that creaks and only two weeks of rehearsal to get everything nailed down. Schedule and budget, that's what they're worried about, not an extra person in the room. Relax."

Trish had expected an empty soundstage, or at the very least a theater setting. Instead, the cast members sat around in plush executive chairs while administrative assistants brought coffee and cappuccino to order. True, the conference table had been pushed to one side and some black electrical tape on the carpet indicated imaginary furniture or blocking marks for the actors. Otherwise, it looked more like a room where lawyers should be consulting than where actors should be creating a summer blockbuster.

At first they just ran lines, sitting comfortably in their chairs. Sometimes Dale let them get through a whole scene. As often as not, he stopped and fine-tuned a reaction or a tone. More than anything, it reminded her of watching spring-training games in baseball. The actors goofed lines, laughed at crucial times, and otherwise screwed up on simple things they'd eventually perform without a hitch later on. Rehearsals were when the cash flowed slowly and they could afford to get tongue-tied or ad lib ridiculous things just because they'd forgotten their lines. Sometimes, it was hilarious.

And sometimes it was enthralling, especially when they began using the blocking marks to actually walk through scenes. Seeing the actors respond to one another not just with dialog but with physical movement brought it alive. It didn't matter that they weren't in costume, that instead of a prop gun, Ty picked up a stapler. What mattered was the reality they created.

Trish couldn't take her eyes off him, the way, in the blink of an eye, he'd inhabit his character. One moment, he'd be smiling at her from across the room. The next, there'd be an aura of danger and unpredictability cloaking him, the sense of a man who could be completely amoral, and yet on whom everything ultimately rested.

Caitlyn was doing an astoundingly effective job of being the young undercover agent lured into a world of decadence. Her character was in Ty's thrall, looking at him as though he were her guide to some mesmerizing place, looking at him as though he were all she could think of.

It didn't matter, Trish told herself. It didn't matter that Caitlyn was beautiful and radiant, it didn't matter that she and Ty were heartbreakingly perfect together. Sure, they'd wind up having an affair once shooting started. How could two people that gorgeous not? Trish knew she was only borrowing good times with Ty. He belonged with a luminous star like Caitlyn. Trish understood it and expected it.

And tried her damnedest to tell herself it didn't matter.

The thing was to stop focusing on the two of them together. She needed to focus on what she was there to do. She needed to focus on the dialog, on how to fix the scenes. She needed to give them wonderful words to say to each other so that they could fall in love.

Her mind shied away at that. The script, she thought. It wouldn't take much, just some adjustments, adding a few lines of dialog. Toughen up the heroine. Don't make her a whiner, make her a strong investigator who's suddenly facing a side of herself that she's never known. Someone caught by a fascination with darkness, a fascination with risk. And Ty's character would be the one to seduce her with the promise of danger. But would he be the real threat, or would her focus on him make her miss the real murderer?

Immersed in scribbling, Trish didn't realize the group had taken a break until she became aware of Ty standing over her. She looked up and flushed. "Sorry, I was in the zone."

"So I see. Can I take a look?" Ty took the pad she proffered and scanned what she'd written.

"It means a shift from the current characters," she explained, "but I think this gives it more edge. Besides, Caitlyn's rep comes from being a fragile flower who rises to the occasion. The goal is not to reinforce that rep but to turn it on its ear, have her play against type."

Ty nodded and skimmed the lines, glancing across the room periodically. "Dale," he called out as the chunky director came back into the room. "Over here."

Dale Westhoff might have been one of the most bankable action directors in Hollywood, but he looked more like a well-fed computer geek who stayed in his dorm room, coming out only for junk food and Star Trek conventions. His hair was a tangled bird's nest, his clothes rumpled; his glasses were perpetually slipping down his nose. He had a reputation for irascibility; she'd already seen he didn't suffer fools lightly.

"Dale, this is Trish Dawson, my assistant."

Dale made a little frown of impatience and ignored Trish's outstretched hand. "We're on the clock here, Ty."

"I thought you'd want to meet Trish. She's the one who wrote the dialog I brought in last week," Ty added.

Now, Westhoff actually turned to look at her. "You did that rewrite?"

"I'm not sure I'd call it a rewrite. It was just a few ideas."

"Never mind," he interjected. "What's your experience?"

Trish shrugged. "I went to UCLA for scriptwriting. Wrote a couple of one-acts. I was the on-staff script doctor for the drama department."

"That new dialog was good work. We're swapping it for the current scene," he added, plucking Trish's annotated script out of Ty's hand without asking and scanning it. He frowned and looked up at her. "So what are you doing here, rewriting the whole damned script? You know, we've already got ourselves a screenwriter."

Her first instinct was to duck, but from somewhere, temper rescued her. "It's not hard to want to edit when you see this script," she said. "I was just entertaining myself. I saw some problems and I had a few ideas on how to fix them."

For the first time, a gleam of humor entered Westhoff's eyes. "That makes two of us. My idea is to use it for kindling. What's yours?"

The corner of her mouth twitched. "I don't believe that for a minute. You know it's a solid story or you wouldn't be working on the project. It's just that the characters need tuning and the dialog needs work."

"Understatement of the year," Westhoff murmured, lapsing into silence as he read.

Trish resisted the urge to say more. All it was likely to do was irritate him. He'd either like it or he wouldn't; it wasn't as if her future was resting on what he thought, anyway. Her eyes met Ty's.

The seconds ticked by and Westhoff turned the pages. At least he was reading and not throwing it down, she told herself. He wasn't the sort to waste time being polite.

Westhoff stirred. "This is good," he said abruptly. "I can see a few things I'd want to tweak, but it's head and shoulders over what we've got now." He glanced across the room to one of his assistant directors. "Jack," he called.

A tall, thin guy with a hipster haircut looked up. "Yo."

"I need my laptop."

Trish looked at Ty, who winked. "You might start canceling your plans for the weekend," he said in an undertone.

She made a face at him.

Jack bustled up. "Here it is, chief."

Westhoff nodded. "Great. Jack, this is Trish, Trish,

this is Jack. I want you to get her set up here with a copy of the script file. She's going to do some work for us. Get her a copy of the production notes, too." He looked back at Trish. "Rewrite this scene first. Put the changes on a disk and the secretary outside will print 'em for you. Let's see how your lines sound with actors reading them." He glanced at his watch. "Okay, five more minutes and we get this show on the road, people."

"So." Ty waited until Dale was gone, then looked at Trish like the cat who ate the canary. "I believe someone was telling me there was no way they'd be allowed even to sit in on rehearsal, wasn't that it?"

"'I told you so's are so tacky."

"Oh, far be it from me to say I told you so. I might, however, mention that we had a little bet riding on the outcome, a little bet that someone just lost."

"A bet?" Trish looked at him blandly. "That wasn't a bet, it was a joke."

"You don't seem like the type to welch on a deal," he commented. "Pay up, Dawson."

A little buzz of excitement ran through her. "Fine. What was it again? A weekend?"

"A weekend as my slave," he finished. "And since today's Friday, I believe it starts in about five hours."

She shot a glance at the ceiling, tongue in cheek. "Fine, if that's what you want."

"If that's what you want, master," he corrected.

THE SUN DIPPED toward the horizon as Ty drove his yellow Boxter up Pacific Coast Highway. Trish glanced at the red-gold stripe the setting sun painted on the blue water. On the inland side, bluffs rose high and sheer. On the other side, the ocean foamed against the rocky coast.

She rode silently beside him. "Do you think Dale meant it, about getting me a contract for the work?" Ty was right, this would mean a guild card, she thought, the first step toward a legitimate career as a screenwriter.

"I can't see why not. Dale might be a little rough around the edges, but if he says he's going to do something, he does it."

The miles whisked by. There was a place in the world for ragtops, she thought, then did a double take. "Hey, wasn't that your turnoff back there?"

Ty moved his shoulders. "Yeah? So? I figured we could get out a little."

He drove until the houses had faded away and the highway was just a ribbon of asphalt winding along the water. It whipped around a curve and dipped between the bluffs and a soaring hummock of rock on the seaward side. His move into the turnout was sudden and practiced.

The sandy, weedy space next to the bluffs might charitably have been called a parking area. Ty stopped the car and turned off the ignition. In the sudden silence, the waves whispered over the ticking of the cooling engine.

"What are we doing?" Trish asked.

"The beach is great in winter. The only people here are the surfers, and they only come out in the mornings, before the offshore wind wrecks the breaks." He opened his door and beckoned to Trish. "Come on, we've been working hard. We've got some time coming."

IT WAS EASY to cross the four lanes through the sporadic traffic to reach the soft sand on the other side. They walked slowly down toward the water. Trish was as relaxed as he'd ever seen her, Ty thought, as he tangled his fingers in hers. The warm light of the setting sun made her skin glow. She laughed as the wind tossed her hair into her eyes and at that instant she was all he'd ever wanted.

He didn't know what it was about her that drew him. Caitlyn Reynolds was the best Hollywood had to offer: attractive, sexy, confident. And yet, when they'd finished rehearsing the seduction scene, when she'd come out of character and given him a smile for him alone, his attention hadn't been on her. The person he'd focused on had been Trish, curled up in a chair in her faded blue sweatshirt, nibbling on the end of her pen.

He'd learned the hard way not to trust his feelings, not to get caught up in the intensity of a scene, the sexiness of a character. He'd learned what love wasn't. How could he now be sure what love was?

And what was it about Trish that caught at his imagination? The contradiction between the assured wanton in his bed and the woman who dressed as though she didn't want to be seen? The fact that he only felt that she was truly his in the moment when he was inside her? The subtle loveliness that flowered into beauty when she smiled, or the wariness that shadowed her eyes?

Perhaps he was just hung up on the challenge.

A seagull soared over the waves, floating on the wind. "I've always envied birds," Trish said. Breaking loose from him, she leaned down to pick up a shell and throw it out over the waves. "I used to have dreams all the time about being able to fly."

Escaping. Always escaping. "Why don't you take flying lessons?" Ty asked, searching out a shell of his own.

She shook her head. "Not the same. You've got an engine making noise. Same thing with a hot-air balloon," she added, before he could ask. "Too many people involved, too much work. I'd just like to take a few steps and jump up and soar."

The globe of the sun touched the water and she shivered. "Maybe we should head out," Ty offered.

They ambled slowly back toward the car hand in hand, listening to the cries of the gulls.

"You know, I don't think I've actually been anywhere with you that wasn't either your house or the production offices," Trish said idly.

Ty shrugged. "Going out somewhere means I become public property."

She raised her eyebrows. "The price of fame?"

"If you like," he said, thinking about the press, the invasions of privacy. "It gets old after a while. I know that the public appearances are part of it all, and I respect that. But that's work. When I'm on my time, I want to be able to kick back, not worry about people talking."

"There's a point where you start being a prisoner in your own life."

"Or what people assume is your life. There are places I can go in Malibu where people are used to actors and don't really think much of it. Anywhere else…" he shrugged. "It's got to be really important for me to bother."

Trish leaned down to pick up a piece of blue-green drift glass. "It's the color of your eyes," she said playfully, the sunlight glinting on her hair.

Ty turned to face her. "I want you to do something for me." Abruptly, he felt a surprising flare of nerves. "The opening at Jocasta's is Tuesday night. I'd like you to go."

"Sure. What do you want me to do?"

He shook his head. "I don't mean go as my assistant. I mean go with me." He gave a brief smile. "As my date."

Her first impulse was to say no, he could see it in her eyes. He wanted to argue; instead, he took her hands, studying her eyes in the last rays of the setting sun.

"You know the press will be there," Trish said uneasily. "Unless I stay in the background, they're going to ask questions, maybe take pictures."

"I don't want you staying in the background."

She didn't trust him, he could see it.

"What about people talking?"

"I also said that when something's important enough, it's worth it." Frustration bloomed then. Suddenly, it seemed that they were talking about much more than just an art showing. "Trish, this opening is important to me. And it's important to me to have you there."

The seconds ticked by. Her fingers were cool in his

as she studied his face. Then she flicked a glance to one side. "I don't have anything to wear."

"Buy something," he said in relief. "We can do it this weekend."

"Oh, no, I'm busy this weekend," she told him.

He frowned. "You've got plans?"

"Someone has plans for me, I believe." She gave him an amused glance. "Master."

He crushed her to him then and sank into the kiss. And driftingly he thought that they might make it.

They just might make it.

TRISH BLINKED at the morning light coming through the blinds of Ty's bedroom window. She was practically living with him, it seemed, going to her apartment to grab clothing or collect the mail. In the space of a week and a half he'd become a fixture in her life, as though he'd always been there.

And would be, at least for now.

She studied him. He'd rolled onto his back and kicked the covers off so that he was covered only by a sheet. Convenient, she thought with a wicked smile, leaning over him. Time to wake him up like a good slave.

She flipped the sheet to one side to expose his body, the long, lean lines of him. God, he was gorgeous. His body spoke of power without seeming muscle-bound, all stripped-down strength and sinew.

The smooth lines and planes begged for her touch, but she fought the temptation. She knew what she wanted, and gazed lower to where his hard-on lay against his belly. It was partially erect with his morning hard-on. Meanwhile, Ty breathed deeply, asleep and unaware of her scrutiny.

Trish licked a fingertip and reached out to stroke the underside of his cock in that little spot just beneath the head where he was most sensitive. A small drop of pre-come eased out the tip as she touched him. He breathed deeper and shifted in his sleep.

Positioning herself until she was close enough to capture him with her tongue, she formed it to a point and drew it up the hard length of him. She stopped and listened to his breathing for a moment to be sure he was still asleep. When his breathing stayed steady, she began again, licking harder this time, tasting the salty nothingness of the pre-come and slicking it down over the hard tip, the velvety soft glans. She brushed her lips against him, and his cock gave a little jump.

It was fully hard now, pulsing a bit against her lips. When it leaped again, she slid it inside her mouth, feeling it thicken and harden as she moved her head, slid all of that heat and warmth up and down the hard length of him. It was intoxicating, this power, this ability to pleasure his body, this ability to learn a man's body in detail.

A week and a half and she was practically addicted.

TY DREAMED OF PLEASURE, of harem girls who stroked his body, brought him erect and to orgasm again and again. Then he felt the silky brush of a woman's hair against his belly and saw a red-haired harem girl slipping his cock into her mouth, sucking on him until he groaned. He tensed and ground his teeth as he tried to hold back from it—

And the translucent curtain of dreams fell away as he swam up toward consciousness.

But the sensation went on. Ty whispered her name, awake now and feeling every nuance of sensation as Trish sucked and stroked and licked at him, now shadowing her mouth with the ring of her thumb and forefinger, now sliding him deep, deep into the warm wetness of her mouth, until he thought he was going to explode.

He reached out to pull at her shoulders and she raised her head. "Good morning, master," she said impudently. "I didn't wake you, did I?"

"I want to be in you," he ordered and brought her up to straddle him.

"You mean like this, master?" she asked, poising her hips over his rock-hard erection.

He moved to ready himself and found her already hot and slick. Sliding up into her was almost enough to take him over, and he gripped her hips for a moment to keep her from moving.

"You're so wet," he murmured.

"You see how much it turns me on to go down on you?" She shifted her hips a little and cradled her breasts in her hands. "What is your wish, my master?"

"I want to see you touch yourself while I'm inside you." When her eyes widened, he reached out to take one of her hands and place it where their bodies met. He moved her fingers a bit and she caught her breath. "Like that," he said.

IT WAS ALMOST MORE than Trish could handle, the feel of him hard inside her, the slow stroke of her fingers held by his. When he released her hand to watch her, his eyes were dark with arousal. If it had turned her on to pleasure him while he slept, that was nothing compared to the sensations rocketing through her now.

Each circle of her fingers took her closer. When he reached out to clasp her hips and raise her up and down, the combination of the two frictions had her crying out. Ty's face was taut with the effort of control. As though he were a wave, she could feel him growing in strength inside her, could feel the moment she pushed them both over into orgasm so that she was quaking and gasping even as he was pulling her down on his cock.

She couldn't imagine how she'd ever done without this feeling.

She couldn't imagine how she would.

11

Trish stood in a corner of Galerie Vizquel, watching the ebb and flow of people. Mostly the flow, she admitted—there wasn't a lot of ebb going on. Outside, a line of people waited to get in; inside, the press milled about with cameras. Ty's pictures hung on the white walls, the images all the more dramatic for the austerity surrounding them. Ty stood to one side, talking with a critic about up-and-coming L.A. artists. A collection of obvious fans formed an adoring half circle around him.

And Trish stood in her red bolero jacket and high-waisted black palazzo pants. Paired with a soft, white silk blouse, it looked like something Katharine Hepburn might have worn—classy, stylish and discreet. She felt at ease and infinitely more comfortable than she'd have felt in any of the short and sexy outfits Cilla had urged her to buy. The choice left her free to stop worrying about herself and watch what was going on, instead.

"I can't believe I'm standing fifteen feet away from Ty Ramsay." A blond woman—girl, really—clutched her girlfriend's forearm, her bracelets jingling. "He's even hotter in real life than he is in the movies. I'm going to try to go up and meet him," she said, fluffing her hair.

"Oh my God, is that Tom Cruise that just came in?" her friend gulped, sounding barely able to breathe with excitement.

"You're so clueless. I can't believe you don't recognize Colin Farrell," the blonde answered, immediately resetting her targeting system.

Trish's lips twitched in amusement. In actual fact, it was neither, but they were already descending on the hapless newcomer.

The room was dotted with the celebrity hounds that Ty had feared, people who spent more time gawking at him than at the art on the walls. There was also the usual handful who stopped in for the scene, not to mention the free drinks and food. A substantial group, though, was there to see what he had done. Trish walked slowly through the room, listening to the bits of conversation.

"…it's a step beyond Beat Streuli or Robert Olsen…"

"…he is an actor, after all…"

"…use of texture creates a tension…"

Indeed, the art world was there in force. It was celebrity hunting of a different sort, Trish supposed, that voracious need to be on the inside track of talent. She wondered what Ty thought.

And how it felt to him to meld his two worlds. When they'd arrived earlier, he'd avoided the front door, directing the driver to let them off in the back alley. "For premieres and awards shows, I'll do the grand entrance. Not for this, thanks."

Jocasta had been waiting for them. She and Ty hadn't greeted one another with an air kiss, but with a genuine hug. It wasn't the contact that caught Trish's attention, it was the obvious affection and the whisper of a connection long past.

Or maybe not so past, Trish thought now, remembering the light in Jocasta's eyes. So severe and stylish it hurt, Jocasta wouldn't be the least amused at being labeled puppyish, but her eyes softened whenever she looked at Ty.

"Quite the feeding frenzy, isn't it?" a voice murmured.

Trish turned to see Jocasta standing next to her in a black sleeveless turtleneck dress that brought out her Josephine Baker eyes. "You got a great turnout. You should be pleased."

"They're certainly buying. I don't know that Ty will be thrilled about the fact that more of them are movie fans than serious collectors, but selling is selling."

"Keeping in business is probably a good thing," Trish agreed, watching Ty shake hands with a critic and in the next move sign an autograph before turning to a woman who looked like a serious art type.

"In this industry? Are you kidding? It's more a miracle, at least when you're starting out." Jocasta waved at someone across the room. "Sometimes I think I'm selling myself as much as selling art."

"That's the way it usually goes," Trish said. "So how long have you been in business?"

"Oh, about five years now. I like to think I've passed the first cut, but I'm not getting too comfortable. I've picked a few up-and-comers before the rest of the pack. I need more, though. When you're small like me, you can afford to take risks that the more established galleries don't have to bother with. If the artists do well, they help you make your name."

"And you help them."

"Of course. That goes without saying."

"I wouldn't think that in this environment it would."

Jocasta turned to study her. "You're smarter than the ones Ty usually falls for. Nice outfit, by the way."

Trish wasn't sure whether to interpret it as an opening salvo or provisional approval. Patronizing provisional approval. Time to move on, she thought. "Well, it's an impressive business," she said, preparatory to leaving.

"I owe a lot to Ty," Jocasta said casually. "He gave me the seed money. Hanging a show for him was the least I could do."

That warranted a response. "Funny, I'd assumed you were hanging his show because you thought he was talented."

"Touché." Jocasta gave her an amused glance. "You don't let much slide, do you?"

"Adequate to the occasion," Trish said equably, smiling at Ty when he looked her way.

Jocasta noticed the glance. Trish had a feeling she didn't miss much. "Ty's talent is a given. Some of my regular customers have followed him for the last couple of years."

Jocasta fell silent as a willowy model type walked in, a woman Trish recognized as Megan Barnes. The same Megan Barnes who'd just broken box-office records as the star of *City of Light*. The same Megan

Barnes who'd been engaged to Ty three years before, she recalled.

Trish watched Ty turn to greet her, pleased that he kissed her on the cheek and not the lips, and frustrated at herself for noticing. Across the room, cameras flashed to capture Megan's sun-drenched California looks, to capture the golden couple reunited.

"Nice of Megan to stop by," Jocasta commented. "That ought to ensure this little soirée makes it into every tabloid. Not exactly what Ty was hoping for. Still, exposure is exposure and I'm sure she means well."

"I'm sure she does," Trish said, exhaling slowly as Megan patted Ty on the arm.

"Ty has a tendency to stay friends with his ex-lovers."

Trish let a beat pass before turning to Jocasta as though she hadn't been paying attention. "Pardon me?"

The fact that Jocasta's smile was kind, was probably the hardest thing to take. "Don't worry, she's probably telling him something that the baby did. Here comes her husband." Jocasta nodded as a dark-haired man with a toothy grin came up behind Megan.

"Ty's one of the good ones," Jocasta continued, "although he might drive you crazy while things are going on. Trust me, he's easier to like once you're no longer sleeping with him."

She wasn't going to rise to the bait, Trish told herself. She wasn't going to rise to that glance that said "I can afford to tolerate you. I've been here through all of them and I'll be here when you're just a memory."

Besides, she was probably right.

"It's unfortunate that he got pulled away by Hollywood," Jocasta said. "He could have been very successful just as an artist."

Trish made a slow survey of the room. "It looks to me as though he already is." She stared across the room at Ty, who beckoned her. "Excuse me."

Jocasta gave her a look as though butter wouldn't melt. "By all means," she said.

TY WATCHED TRISH cross the room to him, the loose, mannish clothing only playing up her femininity. He'd expected her to show up in the usual scene clothes, something short and tight. Then again, she had a way of confounding his expectations. She looked, he thought, like a '40s movie star, with a certain bred-in-the-bone glamour and grace to the way she walked, the way she held herself. It wasn't the kind of showy style that Megan cultivated, for example, and maybe it wouldn't draw the camera lenses, but it made her memorable.

And it made him want her.

She was a continuing riddle to him. She'd been surprised when he'd asked her to accompany him to the opening, as though she'd assumed he'd want a Hollywood escort. As though she'd assumed that they were about no more than sweaty days and nights in his bedroom.

Going out was rarely an option only because it meant sacrificing any degree of privacy and turning the whole thing into a free-for-all. He had a feeling Trish wouldn't be even remotely comfortable with that. Most women outside of the business weren't, which was maybe why he'd tended to get involved with other actors. They knew how it went and they took it in their stride; indeed, some of them, like Megan, for example, thrived on it. Some of them needed the media to verify that they were alive.

Trish didn't seem to be wired that way, so he'd tried to focus on time between the two of them. And yet, there was some part of her that was fragile, unwilling to believe in what was forming between them. It alternately frustrated and perplexed him. How could a woman who looked like she did expect so little? Don't dig, he reminded himself. Better to wait and let her offer it when she felt it was right.

"Hey, you," he said as she came up next to him.

"How's the famous artist?"

Even though he knew it wasn't smart, he couldn't resist leaning down for a kiss. He felt her flinch as the cameras flashed. "Trish, I'd like you to meet Megan Barnes and her husband, John Forrester."

"Pleased to meet you," Megan said warmly. "Sorry to have occupied Ty for so long."

"She had to haul out the baby pictures," John put in. "It's one of those mother's hormone things."

"Mother's hormones, hmmm?" Megan put her tongue in her cheek. "Did you pick up the framed version of the baby picture that you'd ordered for your office, by the way?"

John laughed and pulled his wife close. "All right, I'm outed. It's a parent thing."

The smile that bloomed over Trish's face made Ty

lean over and kiss her again, cameras be damned. There was so much about her that he adored. She was worth his patience. He'd wait her out until she was ready to talk about her secrets. He'd wait her out until she was ready to trust.

TY SAT IN THE BACK SEAT of the limo, holding Trish against him, watching the streetlights strobe over their clasped hands.

"You were quite the success story tonight," she said.

He kissed the top of her head. "We'll see what the critics say. One thing you learn in this town is that what you hear in conversation means nothing. It's what they actually print that counts."

"The show sold out."

"That'll be good for Jocasta," he said carelessly. "It'll let her focus on some other artists. She's good at jumpstarting careers."

"Sounds like she's had some help at it." Trish picked restlessly at his fingers.

So that was why he'd seen the subtle tension in her shoulders when she was talking with Jocasta. "Early on, maybe. She had talent, I had money. Made sense that we combined the two." The tension was back, he realized, though Trish's face was calm. "Did she also tell you we had an affair?"

"She talked like someone who knew you well."

"Not nearly as well as she likes to think. We were involved years ago, before I was acting. We both knew it didn't work." He hesitated, wishing they were talking face to face. Instead, he could only see her expression in profile. "We quit before we tore each other apart. I didn't want to lose what worked with us in the first place, which was art. But there's nothing much outside of that."

"You don't need to explain it, Ty. It doesn't have anything to do with you and me," Trish said calmly.

"Is that a nice way of letting me off the hook?"

"No, it's a nice way of saying I understand we're not serious and I don't have a right to your life."

He shouldn't have been surprised that she would act as though it didn't matter. He didn't want to believe that was the truth. "You sound happy about that."

It stopped her for a moment. "I guess I'm just trying to say that I knew what I was getting into with this and that I don't expect anything out of it."

"Maybe you should." Ty's voice was quiet.

The limo stopped at a light.

"Look, we're having a nice time. Let's just take it for what it is."

"How can you be sure you know what it is?"

BECAUSE SHE KNEW what it couldn't be, Trish thought. "So, have you always pursued your art?" She knew he was looking at her, but she was unwilling to meet his eyes. Couldn't risk it.

Finally, he continued. "Clear through college, I did. Then acting took over. I didn't have the time and I didn't have the energy to do both."

"Understandable."

"Maybe, but unfortunate. You get too caught up in one thing, you get stale, at least I did. After a while, everything was about film and everything was a mess: work, relationships, everything." He paused. "I didn't realize how bad it had gotten until I took a step back and saw all the ways I'd been messing up."

She did turn to look at him then. "You're human. Everyone messes up, you know."

He moved his shoulders. "Yeah, but after a while when you watch yourself making the same mistakes, you start counting up the years and calling it a dead end." He took her hand. "I'm not going to say you're never going to meet ex-lovers of mine, but there's a reason why they're ex. I've put that part of my life behind me. I'm looking for life beyond the movies now." He stared into her eyes. "Do you understand?"

Fatally sincere, she reminded herself. He might think he was telling her the truth. He might actually believe it.

She couldn't afford to.

12

TRISH SAT on the couch, her stockinged feet in Ty's lap and her laptop open on her knees.

"There's got to be a better way to get into this scene than this," Ty said in disgust.

Trish gave him an amused look. "Do you realize you say that every single time we work on a scene?"

"At least I'm consistent."

"Well, I think we're back to the lure of the unknown with this one. I mean, basically, you've got a woman who's only ever indulged in white-bread sex getting talked into letting herself be tied up by someone she has good reason to think is a very dangerous man."

"He's taken her partway there already," Ty pointed out, rubbing her feet.

"And that's exactly what he would leverage," she said, trying to ignore the things his hands were doing to her nerve endings. "He'd go for the incremental strategy. That's what he's been pursuing all along. 'Come on. You've already tried it a bit and it turned you on, didn't it? Admit it. Nobody has to know but me.'"

"We want to avoid the 'you know you want it' thing, though," Ty argued. "That would just make him sound like a jerk."

"That's not what I'm talking about at all." Trish's words trailed off as he slid his fingertips up the inside of her calf.

"Keep going, please," he said with a mischievous glint in his eye. "It's what collaboration's all about. Communication."

Trish moistened her lips. "What we're going for is the whole temptation thing. 'It felt so good to you before, wait until you see how it feels when you really go outside the lines.' She's someone who believes in rules, so breaking them will be twice as much of a turn-on for her. She's getting off on it even though she knows she shouldn't."

Ty brushed his fingers up the inside of her thigh. "Would it be a turn-on for you?"

Her heart began to thud. "If I trusted the person enough. The idea of letting go, really letting go, is amazingly sexy, but also scary as hell."

"Why?" He stroked her skin.

Trish shivered. "Because you leave all of your protection behind. You stop thinking about how you look, how you sound, what the other person thinks."

"The other person thinks that seeing his lover completely lose control because of what she's feeling is an incredible turn-on," Ty told her. "I love touching you and feeling you respond. It's better than having you touch me, even, and that's saying a lot."

Trish caught her breath as she felt the twitch of his hardening cock against the sole of her foot. She remembered the feeling of making love when her hands were bound up in her shirt and lust spurted through her. Did she want to try it? Did she trust him enough?

The certainty was immediate and she set the laptop aside. "Would you want to—"

The buzzer at the front gate rang. They looked at each other. "Are you expecting anyone?" Trish asked.

"Not that I know of."

She rose to check the video monitor in the kitchen. Before she even drew near, she recognized the car and her heart sank. Amber, here to check up on her.

Or to check out Ty.

Trish walked out into the living room and cleared her throat. "Ty, it's my boss." The buzzer rang again, peremptorily.

Ty glanced up from making notes on his script. "You mean your sister?"

Trish bit her lip and nodded. "All right if I let her in?"

"Sure."

She pressed the buzzer for the gate and watched out the kitchen window as Amber drove her black Audi through the open gateway. There was no point in walking straight out to meet her; Amber would need time to fluff her hair and check her lipstick before she'd open the door.

Trish stood on the porch watching Amber get out of her car. "Hello, Amber."

Amber adjusted the belted jacket she wore over a short red skirt that showed her legs to stunning effect. "Good afternoon. I just thought I'd stop in and see how things were going." As she neared Trish, she dropped her voice. "It's been nearly three weeks. You could at least have reported in by now."

"I sent you e-mail and left you voice mail. What more did you want?"

"For you to be dressed in a manner appropriate to representing Amber's Assistants, for one." Amber hissed. "I can't believe you still dress like you're in coll—"

Trish saw Amber's eyes move to look beyond her and she knew.

"God, he's beautiful," Amber breathed.

"You mean our client?"

"Of course our client. I wasn't satisfied with your e-mail. I wanted to see him personally and make sure everything was to his satisfaction. Like the attire of our employee, for example." She gave a pointed look at Trish's sweater and leggings then raised her voice. "Good afternoon, Mr. Ramsay. So nice to meet you in person."

Ty stepped out of the house and crossed the few steps necessary to shake Amber's hand. "It's Ty," he said smoothly. "And you're Trish's sister Amber, right?"

Perhaps if he hadn't been watching carefully, he might have missed her quick frown of irritation. "I'm the president of Amber's Assistants. We like to be sure our customers are satisfied, so I wanted to drop by and check in with you."

"Sure. Why don't you come on in?" He indicated the house, stepping back to allow Trish and Amber to go ahead of him. "Can I get you some coffee? There's some fresh-made."

"I'm sure Trish can get some for us while we talk," Amber said, her heels ringing on the marble tiles.

Ty ignored her. "Come on in the kitchen, we can talk while I get it. What do you take?"

"Cream and sugar, please."

He'd always liked the morning room with its walls of windows. The eucalyptus next to it provided a home for a pair of nesting doves who came back year after year. This late in the season, they were already gone. A pity, he thought, as it meant he had no distractions from Amber.

"Here we go," he said, pouring coffee into his Twentieth Century Fox mug; he figured she'd appreciate it. "Here's the sugar. I hope milk will do." He didn't add that he hoped the milk was also still good, given that he hadn't had a chance to sniff it.

"Trish, if you'd give us some privacy, I'm sure Ty will be more comfortable talking in private."

"I'm fine talking just like this," Ty said mildly. "There's nothing I have to say that Trish shouldn't hear. She's been doing a top-notch job."

"Really." Amber raised a dubious eyebrow.

"Shouldn't be all that surprising to you. You hired her, after all."

It seemed to stop her for a moment. "Yes, well, Trish is quite capable, as you say. We've already discussed her appearance and I can assure you that will be rectified."

"Not if I have anything to say about it."

"Excuse me?" Amber set her coffee mug down.

"Trish takes care of my communications, she's great on the phone, she gets my errands done. And as you can see, casual clothing is fine with me," he said with a tug at his own flannel shirt.

Amber looked as though she'd swallowed a bug. Interesting expression, he thought, noticing Trish was doing her best not to laugh. Eye contact was probably the wrong thing just then, he decided. "Trish has simplified my life, which is what I was looking for. I'm happy with the arrangement all the way around."

"I see."

"Well, I have to get back to work, but I sure appreciate you coming by." He rose, leaving her with little choice but to follow.

"Trish can walk me out, Ty, don't bother yourself."

Like hell was he going to leave her alone with Trish. "It's no bother." But it was the biggest relief he'd had in a while when the engine of the Audi roared to life and he watched her drive away.

"So that's your sister," he said as they walked back into the house.

"That's Amber."

"Is she like that a lot?" He knew it had gotten to Trish. It vibrated all over her.

"Amber's just Amber." She walked in the house ahead of him. "We've got better things to talk about."

Push or wait? For a moment he debated, but the tension in Trish's shoulders decided for him.

"It's true, we do." Ty shut the door. "And can I say that I'm really happy with my luck that of the two of you I got the gorgeous, brilliant, talented and otherwise luscious sister?" he asked, sweeping her in close. The giggle that slipped out of her was music to his ears. He'd been surprised at just how difficult it had been to watch her during Amber's visit.

He gave her a smacking kiss, then lingered. Oh, yes,

and then there was the fact that they'd been so rudely interrupted. He wanted to see where her thoughts had taken her.

He wanted to see if she trusted him enough to try.

"So, what should we do now, work on the script some more, or just take a break?" he asked, then answered his own question by leading her down the hallway. "You started to ask me something before Amber showed up."

"Well, we're having problems with the scene. Maybe we should run through the blocking. Sometimes that can provide ideas," Trish suggested. The tension was gone, he noticed, and in its place arousal and just a hint of daring.

"I've always been a big fan of method acting," Ty observed, stopping at the doorway to his bedroom.

"So have I…master," she whispered, and pulled him inside.

TRISH'S HEART HAMMERED against her ribs as she stripped off the last of her clothing in the afternoon sunlight. He'd been there for her during Amber's visit, he'd stuck up for her in the face of Amber's criticism.

And he hadn't given her sister a second look. She felt connected to him, suddenly, in a way she never had before.

Still, it was one thing to hear Cilla and Delaney talk about the excitement of being tied up by a lover; it was another to actually do it. And yet, the idea aroused her beyond belief. What a paradox it was that the notion of being bound seemed to offer a way to complete and utter freedom.

It all came down to trust.

Ty's eyes were dark with arousal. "Are you sure you want to do this?" he asked, stroking his fingertips along her collarbones.

"It's for research, for the sake of the script." Her voice was unsteady.

He smiled. "Lie back, then."

And now she, the one who'd always lived so quiet a life, was treading the edge, finding out what the limits of her sensuality really were. Trish stretched her arms out toward the bed posts, catching her breath at the soft brush of silk around first one wrist, then the other. She jolted as she felt Ty's fingers curl warm around her ankle.

"Are you comfortable?" he asked.

Trish moistened her lips, aroused with her own daring. "Oh, yes." The soft bond slid around her ankle as he tied it in place. She shivered as he tied the remaining ankle, and then she really was in his control.

Ty settled on the bed beside her, propping his head up on one hand. He stroked his other palm down her ribs, along her waist, over her flat belly. A sheaf of his hair fell over his forehead as he studied her.

Trish's nerves jangled. She'd expected him to tie her up and touch her. She hadn't expected him to simply look and so she fought the self-consciousness. He wanted her. He'd ignored Amber. Here, she thought with a spurt of adrenaline, was where it all came down to trust, the certainty that this was for pleasure, that he would be good to her.

And when she looked into his eyes, as she watched

him watch her, she was certain of it. "You're gorgeous," Ty told her softly, tracing a finger down her neck, over her chest, and to the point of one nipple. Trish tried to move her hands to touch him—

And came up against the limits of her bonds.

"Patience," Ty reminded her, circling his tongue in closer to her nipple. "Don't worry about touching, just feel."

It was harder to trust that arousing her was enough for him, she discovered abruptly. She felt as if she should be doing more. She wanted to move and all she could do was hold still, quivering under his touch.

"Feel how hard I am," he whispered, pressing his cock against her. "This turns me on so much, watching you get turned on." He pulled her nipple into his mouth.

The warmth, the heat tore a moan from her. Ty felt the skin tighten into a stiff little bud and worked to level his system. He wanted to see her let loose, to feel her abandon herself to pleasure. Part of him was desperate to drive deep into her hot softness and spill himself, but he knew he'd be sorry after. Better to prolong the experience, to stretch out the anticipation until he was grinding his teeth in a battle for control.

All the more arousing to see how far he could take her into utter ecstasy.

"Close your eyes."

"Yes, master," Trish whispered. Arousal vaulted through her. And like the fragility of a butterfly's wing, something brushed over her cheek. It wasn't the touch of lips or tongue but something softer, silk perhaps? Light as a breath, it stroked down her arm, leaving a trail of goose bumps in its wake. A moment later, it brushed up her other arm, stroking, caressing, even as Ty's lips moved against hers, pulling her into a deep, slow kiss. He pulled away before she was ready, leaving her waiting, heart pounding, for the next sensation.

When it came, it wasn't the brush of silk but the light scrape of teeth over her nipple, and the trail of his tongue down her quivering belly toward where she ached to feel him. Then it was gone, even as she shifted against him.

Seconds ticked by.

Something cool and smooth brushed up her calf, trailing its way up the inside of her thigh. It no more than reached the top before it was slipping down her other leg. Trish shivered. She fought the urge to open her eyes, testing herself. *Trust.* The touch trailed up over her hip, along the curve of her waist, and over to swirl around the tender skin of her breasts, brushing her nipples until she moaned.

Ty slid it up her neck to her cheek and she caught a hint of fragrance. The rose that he'd brought home from Jocasta's opening and placed in the bathroom. The flower petals slowly caressed her belly, then lower still, circling around the area between her legs. Then they stroked up in between and she jolted.

The mattress gave as Ty got onto the bed beside her. Trish made an impatient noise. "Touch me," she pleaded in a strangled voice.

"All right." Instead of stroking her where she burned for it, though, he ran his hands up over the fragile skin between her breasts, then along her collarbones and up her neck. She had never dreamed that a touch there would tighten the coil of tension between her thighs. Suddenly, her entire body felt connected, all of it tied to the arousal that gripped her. All of it tied to him.

And then, when she least expected it, when she was still buzzing with the last touch, his fingers found her. Trish cried out and her body bucked, but he'd moved on even as the sensation carried her. The briefness of the contact made it all the more vivid. Anticipation had her strung tight as a wire. It was an exquisite intensity beyond that of normal lovemaking. It was giving up control that had brought her to this point, the point where her whole world was built around the promise of his touch.

And when his tongue found her, hot and quick, it sent her fighting against her bonds, crazy with the urge to have her hands on him. Heat, liquid and smooth, stroked in maddening patterns over her clitoris, building the tension until she was ready to scream with it. Minutes passed until she was so close to orgasm that she no longer heard her moans, no longer realized the rhythmic pump of her hips. But just as she started the rushing slide to glory, he pulled away again.

"Please," Trish called out raggedly.

Before she could draw breath, Ty slid up, over and into her with a suddenness that caught and held her. And that quickly, his restraint was gone. She could feel him, fully aroused, pumping in and out of her in a frenzy as his body surged against hers. It was true what he'd said, that watching her pleasure brought him to a fever pitch. She could feel it in the thick hardness of his cock, hear it in the tortured gasps of his breathing.

She could feel it in the pleasure that began in her body and ended in his. Every fiber of her being concentrated on the insistent stroking and heavy pressure, taking her up and up, building to a level she'd never imagined she could reach. And when it flung her into jolting orgasm, in wave after wave, the sensation flowed over her. Each time she thought she was nearly finished, she'd rise to another peak until she cried out with amazement. Until she cried out his name.

13

A BRISK WIND whisked the leaves around the courtyard at Park La Brea, sending them skittering along the footpaths. "This is a banner moment," Ty observed as he walked up to Trish's front door.

"What do you mean?"

He looked at her. "I finally get to see where you live. Always before you've just kind of disappeared for a couple of hours and come back with clothes. I started wondering if you were hiding a husband or something over here."

"Come on in and find out," she invited, and opened her front door.

After the days and nights spent at Ty's house, walking into her apartment was a shock. The place looked unfamiliar, as though she were intruding in someone else's home. It wasn't someone else's home, though, it was hers.

Trish had been thrilled when she'd moved in. Though it had taken her years to get the look right, she thought, admiring the beveled mirror she'd picked up at a desert flea market, but it held together. Even compared with the stretched-out space of Ty's house, it had its own style. She just had to get used to it again.

"I like it," he commented, dropping Trish's overnight bag to the floor. Almost casually, he reached out an arm and scooped her in. "I like the tenant even better," he murmured.

Trish leaned in for a quick kiss that stretched out into long minutes. "Mmm," she said when she finally pulled away.

"Mmm, indeed. Why don't you come over to the couch, here, and we can discuss that part further?"

He had an unerring skill for making her resolve melt away. "We came here to get some clothes for me and then we've got to go over your closing scene," she said, easing away from him.

"We've already finished it. You polish too much."

"I polish just enough, and I think we should take another look," she said. "We have to do it today. Filming starts in less than a week."

"Slave driver."

"I only want what's best for you, dear," she said in a bright and shiny tone, patting his cheek.

Ty strolled over to the couch and flopped down. "What's best for me on a Saturday is forgetting about work and making love with you. Besides, we haven't christened your bed."

And if she had her way, they wouldn't. Ty was going to leave too big a gap when things were over as it was. She didn't want the memory of his beautiful face against her pillows haunting her. Trish hung her purse over the back of a chair. "I'm going to go grab the mail. I'll be back in a sec and we can go."

Given that she hadn't been back for nearly a week,

her box was probably stuffed to capacity, she thought as she walked over to the mail kiosk.

"Oh, there you are. I haven't seen you in so long I was wondering if you'd moved." Trish turned to see Ellie twinkling at her, white hair pulled by the wind into disarray. The velour track suit this time was mauve, and its wearer looked primed for gossip. Trish's heart sank. "Hi Ellie, how have you been?"

"Just fine. And you?"

"Dandy." Trish pulled out her keys and unlocked the little door of her mail slot.

"I guess it has been a while," Ellie said, her bird-bright eyes noticing the mail wedged in Trish's box. "I saw your young man. He's quite a handsome one."

"Now, stop that," Trish scolded. "He's just a friend."

"He seemed like a very attentive friend to me. But wait," she put a hand on Trish's arm. "Don't run off just yet. Let him cool his heels a bit. Anyway, I need to tell you about Mr. Fox getting locked out of his apartment. You wouldn't believe the way the new assistant at the rental office treated him. He's been renting here for almost forty years and she demanded I.D.…."

And she was off and running, leaving Trish standing there blinking in the sunlight.

TY SPRAWLED ON THE COUCH, looking over the apartment. Trish had a sense of detail that manifested itself in small ways: the paperweight on the end table, the trio of vases on the hearth, the twisting columns of candles on the coffee table. The furniture was deep and soft, in luxuriant colors like dark purple and dark green. The women he dated usually lived in houses with that "professional decorator" look, houses with just the right angles and objets d'art cast casually about. This space had none of that professional patina. It was clearly all Trish, acquired piece by painstaking piece with an eye for form and style.

His cell phone burbled for attention. Carelessly, he pressed the "end call" button that sent the caller to voice mail. Before he could turn it off, the phone burbled again. He glanced at the display to see Charlie's number. Ty grinned and flipped it open. "I told you, I don't want to buy a timeshare in Cancun. Now stop calling."

"Funny. Ramsay, why don't you answer your phone?"

"I just told you. Besides, why should I talk with you and ruin my day?"

Charlie snorted. "While you're lying around being a big movie star, some of us are power-brunching."

"Really? Making waffles for the kiddies?"

"My waffles are legendary, you know."

"I'm sure."

"That being said," Charlie said thoughtfully, "the last time we used the waffle iron it fused shut. I thought I'd be nice and let a professional make them today. Went to The Ivy."

"How were the waffles?" Ty reached out to pick a green glass cube off the coffee table.

"Not nearly as good as the company. You'll never guess who I wound up sitting next to while we were waiting for a table."

"I'm guessing you'll tell me."

"None other than Mr. Indie, Paul Tate. I met him last year at Sundance."

Ty considered, holding the cube up to his eye to look through it. "I suppose this is my cue to ask what you talked about."

"Very good," Charlie said approvingly. "We chatted about a little of this, a little of that. He was going on about how he couldn't find anything worth sinking his money into right now."

"Sad thing."

"Isn't it just," Charlie agreed. "Seemed like a good time to bring up GDI."

"And?"

"We have ourselves one very interested fellow. He liked the idea of having your pretty face involved."

Ty sat forward, setting the cube aside. "Not to mention my pretty wallet."

"Hey, if we can get him to pony up some money on a film, we'll be doing the happy dance."

"My feet are twitching already. So what happens now?"

"He wants to talk with you and then maybe arrange a meet."

It was funny how just the promise of their company had him more excited that the reality of his current film. "He wants a meeting, he's got one. Tell me when and where."

"I'm going to give you his phone number. Write this down."

"Just a minute." Ty scanned the room and walked to

a spindle-legged deco desk against one wall. There had to be a scrap of paper he could use. The pens were easy to find, all stuffed in a pewter vase. Paper, there was in abundance, though it mostly was computer printouts, he realized, moving it just enough to see if there was anything usable underneath.

Then he took a closer look.

"While I'm still young, Ty?" Charlie said.

"You were born an old man," Ty replied automatically, picking up the clipped-together stack of paper on top. It was a script, he realized, scanning it. A finished script.

With Trish's name on it.

There was no reason for him to be surprised, really. If she had a talent for revising scripts, why wouldn't she be writing one of her own? Except that when he'd asked her about it she hadn't told him.

The stab of disappointment was sharp and vicious.

"Ramsay?"

"Look, I'm not at home. Can you just leave the number on my answering machine? I'll call him as soon as I get in." Suddenly, GDI Films receded in importance. Instead, there was the script, something Trish had obviously invested time, energy, effort in. The few lines he read rang true. She had to have been working on it well before they'd gotten involved, and yet she'd never said a word about it. Hidden it, to be honest.

She'd never trusted him at all.

"Okay, I'll leave the number, but let me know what happens."

"You'll be the first," Ty promised absently and switched off the phone.

Then he picked up the script and settled on the couch to read.

HER HEAD SPINNING from the gossip dump and her arms filled with mail, Trish opened the door to her apartment. "Ty?"

Ty raised his head and gave her an opaque look. "I was thinking maybe you'd run off."

Trish crossed to pile the mail on the kitchen table. "Chatty neighbors," she said by way of explanation. Then she noticed the sheaf of paper in his hands. "What are you reading?" she asked sharply.

"What, this?" Ty held out the paper and she snatched it from his hands. "Maybe you can tell me. It looks an awful lot like a script."

"I can see that." The sense of invasion was sharp and strong, the need to protect, immediate. "Who gave you permission to snoop?"

"Snoop? I got a phone call," he said evenly. "I was looking for a piece of paper to write something on. And funny thing, there it was."

He was pissed, Trish realized with a little twist of anxiety. Then again, so was she. "You must have done some looking. I had it covered up."

"Yeah, the stapler on top was pretty effective. I almost missed it," he returned. "Like I said, I was looking for paper."

"So you started digging through my stuff and just figured you had a right to read anything you saw?" She heard the edge in her voice and didn't care.

"Well, since I'd been told it didn't exist, I guess I wasn't sure what it was." Ty went to the window and looked out into the courtyard. "Were you ever going to tell me about it?" He turned back to her.

Trish balled her hands in her pockets. "I don't know," she answered, wishing desperately that this hadn't come up, that she'd tucked the script safely away in a drawer. "It's not that easy, considering the circumstances."

"What circumstances?" His temper flared. "The fact that we've spent almost every minute together for the last three weeks either talking or making love? There's a point where you start to trust me, Trish, isn't there? *'What are your dreams, Ty, what do you want?'* It's okay to grill me about my art and how I feel about it, but you don't tell me anything? You'd even lie?"

"I didn't lie to you."

"No, you just changed the subject every time it came up. Like you do about a lot of things, come to think of it."

That was it, she realized. He'd opened up to her and she'd held out on him. And yet, how could she have told him?

"You know, I'm a pretty patient person," Ty went on, dragging a hand through his hair. "I keep thinking that you'll start talking at some point, that you'll really start talking to me about the things that matter to you. I know what it's like to put your heart into something and hope that it's good. I understand how hard it is to put it out there. But after all we've done together? Hell, writing a script shouldn't be a state secret by now. My God, half the people in L.A. are doing it."

"And you dismiss them just like you'd have dismissed me if you'd known about it. Another wannabe. If I'd told you, you'd have been thinking, 'Great, now she's going to ask me to help her out.' Admit it," she snapped, "you would have."

"The first day you met me, maybe," he admitted, "but now? You're working on the *Dark Touch* script, for chrissakes."

"An action script."

Ty bristled. "An action script that's actually getting produced. You don't need to remind me that it's not Shakespeare."

"That's not what I meant and you know it. It's a different type of film altogether. Anyway, I'm just editing it, it's not like coming up with your own thing from scratch." She paced away and whirled to face him. "What am I supposed to say to you, anyway? We're having sex, now read my script? The same as every other Hollywood hopeful who gets within ten paces of you, probably."

His gaze hardened. "Despite what you apparently think, I don't sleep with everyone who comes within ten paces of me. And in case you haven't noticed, what we've been doing the last couple of weeks isn't just about sex. Or at least that's what I've been thinking." He stalked toward her. "Unless I've just been an idiot all this time."

Fatally sincere, she thought. "We're not involved," she protested. "I'm not a fool, Ty."

"Goddammit." His voice rose in frustration. "What have I got to do? What's it going to take for you to trust me?"

"I can't afford to trust you," she said passionately. "It's not going to last, and we both know it."

"We both know it? I don't know anything except that you're always in the starting blocks. You talk about me being ready to bail, but you're the one who's set to run."

"I'm not like Megan and Jocasta and all the other women you sleep with," she retorted. "I don't have an art gallery or a big movie career. I can't keep up with them. And I'm not going to pretend I can."

"I'm not asking you to. All I want is for you to be yourself—if you'll give me some idea of who that is. I don't want to keep talking about me all the time and I want to know more about you than what I can find out in bed. But you're so busy guarding yourself that you don't have time for anything else."

"Stop pushing me!" She blinked furiously even as her eyes filled. "Why should I let you in when you'll just walk away."

He crossed to her. "Who says I'm going anywhere?"

Trish put her hands up. "Don't, all right? Don't." Her voice shook.

"At least sit down," he murmured, drawing her to the couch. And then he did gather her close, despite her protests, stroking her hair and shushing her. It twisted his heart to feel her quake against him and know it was tears, not passion. "Tell me what's going on," he said softly. "Tell me."

And she did. The afternoon shadows stretched out as she told him about life with Amber, life as a high-school misfit. About her first crush, the guy who she thought had liked her until she realized he was only walking her home in the hope of meeting Amber. And she told him about going to college and falling totally and completely in love her first semester in the dorms.

Brett Spencer had been like a special prize she got for finally outgrowing her baby fat and becoming thin and pretty like Amber. He flirted, he encouraged, and if he never made a major move, he always left her feeling like the next time they met, it would happen. She remembered the wonder of feeling that she was finally wanted. And then the intimacy and magic of the night before Christmas break, the painful surprise of sex, and the incredulous knowledge that she, Trish, finally had a lover.

But the new year had held surprises of its own.

"I'd come up from San Diego the night before the dorms reopened to go to a Filter concert. I'd asked Brett to come with me. We were supposed to stay over at his parents' house, but they lived out in Oxnard, too far to drive, so he'd asked his dorm buddy Drew if we could sleep over at his house. Drew's parents were on vacation, so a bunch of his friends were staying over anyway."

She remembered the excitement of seeing Brett after the long holiday break, and the puzzlement she'd felt. "I couldn't figure out what was wrong when I saw him again, but it was different somehow," Trish said slowly. "He barely touched me. Then again, he never had before, so I didn't know if I was expecting too much. Maybe that was how it was, what did I know?"

After the concert, they'd gone back to Drew's house and stretched out in sleeping bags on the living-room floor, Trish miserably uncertain and uncomfortable. "It was so weird to be in someone's house like that to start with. I'd drifted off, I guess, and when I woke up, Drew was home with a couple of friends and Brett was out at the kitchen table with them, playing quarters."

And it made her cringe to remember.

"Then they started talking about me. The guys were ribbing Brett about me, saying I was his little puppy dog, that I was at his beck and call. I wanted to leave, but we'd brought all my stuff in from my car because of the concert, and it was stacked in a corner. Anyway, San Diego was a three-hour drive away." Remembered anxiety tightened her voice and Ty kissed her hair gently.

"Anyway, it got worse," she continued. She'd closed her eyes, miserably hoping they would stop so that she could pretend it hadn't happened. Instead, they'd gotten drunker. "The more beer they had, the meaner they got, especially Brett. He told them he'd only brought me along because he wanted the concert ticket, that he'd only slept with me before Christmas because Drew had locked him out of their room." The night that she'd been giddy and overwhelmed with love. Trish remembered how it had felt to finally kiss him, the knowledge that they'd spanned the gap. And it hadn't mattered that the sex had been awkward and uncomfortable because it had been with him, because she was in love with him, and she'd have done anything for him.

But he'd only done it to have a place to sleep.

"Drew was a nice guy and kept trying to stop him.

And Brett was saying things about how I'd been in bed…" She couldn't make herself say them aloud. Like a dead fish he'd said. Gave a blow job like she'd never seen a cock before. His barbs had drawn steadily louder laughter, even as Trish had twisted in silent humiliation. "And then he said that he was tired of dealing with me."

He'd flirted with her because it had amused him. He'd gone to the concert with her merely to get a ticket. And he was talking now, cruelly and publicly, because he wanted her gone.

She had gotten up, then, face burning, to grab her purse and walk out the door. They'd tried to stop her, she recalled, but she'd ignored them all and driven into the night. It hadn't just been shattered love, it had been the embarrassment, being publicly used and publicly ridiculed. It was life as it had always been—not pretty enough, not sexy enough, not adept enough.

Not good enough.

She'd wept and roved the network of L.A. freeways before exhaustion got the better of her. Only then, at 2:00 a.m. had she realized that she had nowhere to go. She didn't have the money for a hotel. Driving home wasn't an option—it would practically be morning by the time she reached San Diego, and how would she explain what she was doing there?

Finally, in desperation she'd driven up Interstate 5 to a truck stop north of L.A., and locking her doors, half panicked, she'd dozed until morning. It had taken all of her strength, but she'd driven back to Drew's, loaded up her car without a word, and returned to the dorms.

And swore never to put her heart in the hands of another.

Ty was silent for a long time after she'd finished. "You know he was an idiot, right?" he said finally. "It wasn't you."

Trish moved her shoulders. "I didn't have anything to compare it to. Things like that happen, they're pretty hard to forget. Anyway, that next semester I met the rest of the gang in the Supper Club. I live vicariously through them."

"I hope the next guy got him out of your mind."

She was silent a moment before answering. "It probably doesn't sound like that big a deal, but you can't imagine what it was like to sit there and hear all those things. I'd been crazy about this guy, and hearing him brag about how he'd used me, hearing him ridicule me? I walked out of there never wanting to have a thing to do with any guy ever again."

Ty tightened his arms around her. "It can be different now," he said softly.

"It's hard to believe that. It sticks with you."

"How about if you just believe in me?" he asked. The afternoon had faded as they'd talked and her face was shadowed now and hard to read. What would it take to break past the old hurts? he wondered.

A person who'd had a normal dating life would have chalked the whole thing up to a bad experience, but someone without any basis for comparison? And what about the comments she'd made about growing up as the ugly duckling? That might have explained the dull clothing, the instinct to hide. "You're incredible. I've never met anyone like you." He turned her face to his and kissed her gently. "Trust me, Trish. I won't hurt you."

"You can't guarantee that," she said bleakly. "No one can."

"What can I do?"

She leaned her forehead against his. "Just be with me, Ty," she murmured. "Just be with me now."

This time things weren't going to get out of hand, Ty thought. This time they were going to go slow and easy. This time he was going to give to her.

To give to them both.

Soft kisses, slow strokes, touches that said "believe in me." When he picked her up and carried her to the bedroom, it wasn't for drama's sake, it was because it seemed right to cradle her in his arms, to take care of her. How it would end, he couldn't know, but he could control the now. He could make her feel treasured.

Her body was long and lovely in the late-afternoon light. When she moved to satisfy him, he pressed her back against the white sheets. "Not tonight," he whispered. "This is for you."

And dreamily, she let him take her up. In the morning, she might be embarrassed that she'd opened up the dark places in her soul to him; tonight, he could only be grateful that she was letting him wipe it all away with gentleness, treating her as though she were rare and precious.

Even when he brought her to her peak, it was tender. And when he slipped inside her and began moving, the journey was as important as the destination.

TY WOKE, BLINKING in the darkness. Trish was a warm bundle beside him, one of her arms carelessly thrown across his chest in sleep.

If he'd had a chance, he'd have throttled the idiot from college, but he knew that wouldn't really have done it. That jerk had just reinforced everything she'd grown up feeling. It was her bad luck that it had happened as it had, that instead of finding someone honest who'd make her feel good about herself, she'd gotten hooked on the one person who would hammer the point home even more strongly.

The strange dynamic with Amber made a lot more sense, too. Among his own sisters, the pecking order was clear and established. He'd assumed that that was part of what was in place. Now, he realized, it was about much more. Amber was busily keeping Trish in the place she'd always been, in the place that made Amber most comfortable—the place that would allow her to feel superior.

The problem was that Trish was letting her do it. Sure, she stood up for herself a little, but she didn't lay down the law. It wasn't his to do, though, and he doubted talking about it would help. It was a path she had to find on her own.

She'd been taught not to expect anything. It frustrated him, but it explained a lot. His own track record made him easy for her to dismiss. Certainly, a year before when he'd emerged, shell-shocked, from his last relationship, he'd expected to take more time figuring things out.

Sometimes life ran contrary to your expectations.

He pulled Trish closer in the dark and kissed her forehead. Sometimes, he thought, and he smiled.

14

TRISH OPENED her eyes, registering the fact that she was in her own bedroom at the same time as she felt the warmth of Ty's arms around her. And she thought back to the night before and squirmed mentally. What had she been thinking, telling him about Brett, telling him about being the overweight outcast in high school? Someone as beautiful as Ty wouldn't understand not fitting in. All she'd done was brand Loser on her forehead. She wanted to slap herself.

Instead, she wriggled to the edge of the bed. Ty held on to her at first, releasing her with a murmur and rolling over to slide back into sleep. She crept to her closet and pulled out clothing. Then she slipped out the bedroom door, closing it behind her.

She didn't really relax, though, until she was dressed and stepping into the morning air. The sun was showing through the translucent cloud cover, hinting that the overcast would burn off into a sunny day. It was unseasonably warm for October. Of course, northerners probably considered the depths of L.A. winters to be always unseasonably warm, as far as that was concerned.

She crossed Sixth Street to reach the park. Sidewalks wound over the broad lawns, playground equipment sat on tanbark. The County Museum of Art was closed, which was fine with her. She wasn't in a mood to be enclosed anywhere.

Forget about art, the La Brea tar pits before her were probably a better fit for her state of mind. A concrete ramp led up to a viewing area that overlooked one of the oily pools of tar. The curators had added fiberglass animals to help visitors understand what had happened at the pits thousands of years before.

A mastodon sagged in the pool, up to its fiberglass shoulders in tar, its trunk flung up in alarm. She knew how it felt. She, too, had stumbled into something that was deeper and stronger than she'd ever expected, and now she was out of her depth.

She put her head down against the metal railing, rolling her forehead back and forth. Small chance she could expect him to forget what she'd told him, but perhaps she could ignore it and go on.

She could pretend until pretending wasn't necessary any more.

TY WOKE ALONE, reaching out to find the bed beside him empty and cool. With a yawn, he rose, not bothering with clothing. "Trish?" The apartment was small; it didn't take long to figure out she was gone. It didn't surprise him; what surprised him was the surge of frustration and disappointment. He'd thought they'd made progress the night before. Clearly, it wasn't enough.

Every time he thought he was getting closer to breaking down her walls, he'd blink and find them stronger than ever. Maybe he was a fool to keep beating his head against them, but some part of him was convinced that eventually he'd pull them down. Patience, he told himself as he dressed. She needed patience and time. Maybe then she'd come around.

He roamed around the apartment, seeking clues. Her purse was still in evidence, so wherever she'd gone, she hadn't driven. Her jacket had disappeared, so she probably hadn't just gone to the workout center. Beyond that, he hadn't any idea where she might be.

Ty moved restlessly around the living room. Passiveness didn't come naturally to him, but neither did foolishness. If he went wandering around outside, she might return while he was gone and they'd be no better off than before. Instead of looking for her, perhaps he'd be better off having a cup of coffee or reading.

Or, he thought, picking up the binder-clipped stack of paper from the coffee table, he could look at her script.

He settled down to read, and didn't notice the time pass. Had she realized how much of herself she'd put into the script? he wondered. How much of Callie's yearning and fears were just elements of Trish? She'd told him some things about herself the night before; reading her script told him more.

He stared into space for a moment. Through the picture window he could tell where the first fitful beams of sunlight were finally shining through the overcast. A sunny day… Thoughtfully, he punched numbers into his cell phone and spoke briefly to the person on the other end, then lapsed back into reading.

Finally, the sound of the key in the lock made him glance up. Trish stood in the doorway. For a moment, he just looked at her, studying the tension in her frame, the strain in her face.

"Hi." She shut the door behind her.

"Having a nice morning?"

"I went for a walk."

The clock showed nearly ten; he'd been up for two hours and she'd been long gone. "I scrounged for some coffee. I hope you don't mind."

Trish gave him a guilty look. "I'm sorry I took so long. I guess I should have left you a note."

"I've been keeping myself entertained." Ty studied her reaction to his reading material. Nerves, he noticed, but no anger.

She stood, ill at ease, and finally walked over to perch on the couch by him. "So what did you think?"

"It's good. Really good."

"Seriously?" She made eye contact with him for the first time. "Don't say it just to be nice."

"I'm never nice," he said severely, then leaned in to kiss her thoroughly.

She was dazey-eyed when he released her. No better time, he decided. "I want to show the script to a couple of people. I want to play Michael."

It took a minute to sink in, then the shock hit. "Michael? But he's…he's…"

"Not an action hero?"

"Yes. No. I mean, it's not the kind of thing you do."

"That's precisely why I should do it. I'm sick of playing the same character in different clothes all the time."

"It's just that I've always imagined it as an Indie production, not something that a person like you would star in."

It stopped him for a minute. "I'm going to take that as a reference to my asking price rather than a knock on my acting skills." He didn't want it to be, he so didn't want it to be, because he wanted her to believe in him.

Because he already, in that brief span of time, longed to be Michael.

Ty weighed the script in his hand. "Besides, the person I'm thinking of showing this to is a buddy who directs Indie films. We're trying to get a production company together."

She frowned. "Don't do me any favors."

"Trust me," Ty said, "I'm not. We're considering a number of scripts. I'm just adding yours to the bottom of the list. Anyway, we've got to get funding or nothing goes forward."

Mollified, she subsided.

"So does that mean you'll let me take this and make a copy?"

She considered. "Don't you have an assistant to do that for you?"

"You're right," he said in amusement. "I do."

Trish stared at him, trying to take it all in. Getting her script made into a film was the stuff dreams were made of. And yet, she felt a little as she imagined a mother might feel at sending a child off to her first day of kindergarten: a wish to see her offspring sprout its wings and fly and a yearning to keep it safely to herself. There was no glory in safety, though. "I'll make a copy tomorrow morning. You can show it to whoever you like."

"Great." He kissed her. "Now let's take a shower and get going."

"Where to?"

"You'll see."

WHATEVER SHE'D EXPECTED, it hadn't been this. She hadn't expected him to drive for over an hour. She hadn't expected him to head northeast into the Antelope Valley and toward the heart of the desert.

Even in October, it was warm, and the clouds thinned as they drove until the sun came out and she was glad of her dark glasses. Gradually, the landscape emptied out, turning sere and bleached. Creosote bushes and sage grew in tufts off the road; high above flew a white spot that might have been a plane.

Her first clue to where they were going came when he pulled off the highway near Palmdale and passed a white sign off the road that said Desert Soarers. The complex just past it proved to be a small airstrip, with a collection of Beechcrafts and Cessnas sitting on the tarmac apron.

"Wake up, we're here." He got out of the car. She heard a clunk as the trunk opened.

"What is this?"

Ty pulled on a royal blue sweatshirt that made his eyes glow. "A present." He walked around to where she stood next to the car and kissed her. "Happy Sunday. You said you'd always wanted to be a bird."

On the apron in front of them sat a small blue Cessna—and strung up to it by a cable, a wasp-waisted glider, white as a gull. Trish's eyes went round. Did it really take so little? he wondered.

"You're taking me up in a glider?"

"I looked into plastic surgery to graft wings onto you, but I couldn't find anyone who would hollow out your bones on short notice."

Something tightened in her chest. "I can't believe you even remembered that I said that."

"We actors are taught to pay attention to detail," he said as Trish gave him an enthusiastic kiss. "Particularly when it pays dividends."

She laughed and ran over to the glider, Ty following behind. The aircraft's body was sleek and smooth, its long, graceful wings dwarfing those of the Cessna, which looked like a Shetland pony next to a thoroughbred by comparison.

A mechanic in coveralls, his graying hair caught back in a ponytail, looked up from checking the fuel in the Cessna. "Ramsay, when are you going to spring for a motor glider and stop wearing me out towing you?"

"Hoyt, you don't know what to do with yourself when you're not in the air," Ty said good naturedly. "Besides, it ain't soaring if it's got an engine, even if you do turn the damned thing off."

"I like a man who's a purist." Hoyt winked at her. "So, you going to introduce me to your lady friend?"

"Hoyt Trotter, Trish Dawson. If Hoyt doesn't know it about a plane, it's not worth knowing," Ty said to her.

Hoyt wiped his hand on his leg and held it out to shake. "A pleasure. You ever been up in one of these babies before?"

"No, but I'm looking forward to it."

"Watch out or you'll get hooked. Next best thing to having wings." A warm gust of wind sent sand scattering over the tarmac. "You've got a good day for it," he said with a nod.

Ty helped her find the steps to get into the cockpit. The seat wrapped around her snugly. With the Plexiglas dome, Trish felt like some sort of astronaut.

Ty slipped into the seat ahead of her and excitement jittered in her stomach. The Cessna started to roll. A smooth acceleration, a tilt, and in a breathless second they were airborne.

Trish watched the ground fall away. She could hear the roar of the Cessna's engine, but the glider followed smoothly. To the north, the Tehatchapi Mountains were shrouded in haze, as were the San Gabriels; to the east, the desert stretched away into emptiness.

"I didn't know you flew," she said, surprised at how well her voice carried in the cockpit.

"I don't. It's called soaring."

She gave an instant laugh. "So once we cut loose, we coast back to the airfield?"

"Nope. Once we cut loose, the fun's just starting."

The altimeter number ratcheted up. Below them, the desert spread out, fading to bluish haze at the margins.

"Okay, you ready?"

An unholy excitement spun in her stomach. One minute they were attached to the minute vibrations of the Cessna. The next, Ty had released the tow cable and they were floating free. Hoyt dipped his wings and cut away below them, leaving them alone. The engine noise faded away, leaving an eerie silence augmented only by the whisper of the glider's canopy through the air.

"Now you're going to see why they call it soaring," Ty said, turning the glider toward a darker area. Suddenly, her stomach lurched; they were buoyed up as though raised by an invisible palm.

"What was that?" she yelped.

"Thermals. That's what soaring is all about. The tow just gets you started, you can ride the thermals as long as there's sun."

He brought the glider around in a lazy arc, nudging it toward the foothills of the Tehatchapis.

"This is wonderful!"

"Like Hoyt said, 'it's the next best thing to having wings.'"

It was amazing to her that this floating sensation was driven by nothing more than warmth, than nature itself. She felt free in a way she never had in her whole life. The land was spread out below, the mountains like a rumpled coverlet, the desert fading into sky at the horizon. It was like the dreams she'd had of soaring along. She remembered a poem she'd heard once, about slipping the surly bonds of earth to fly. The ground seemed a forgotten place; this was where she belonged.

Ty rapped on the canopy and pointed off the left wing. And there, riding the thermal with them, was a hawk, its tail a flash of red. It looked at them. She'd swear it looked directly at them, curious and unafraid, then banked and was gone.

Trish gazed out then at space and openness and air. He'd given this to her, she realized suddenly. He'd given her this extraordinary experience, all because of something she'd laughingly said on a beach. He'd known her well enough to realize what it meant.

And Ty caught the knife-edge thermal from the ridge of a sheer cliff, sending them up ever higher.

Together.

THE SOLID GROUND under her feet didn't seem real. It felt like a temporary stopping-over place until she could go up again. Immediately, she understood why Hoyt might live in this godforsaken desert town, do whatever he had to do to keep flying.

"I love it! I love it! I love it!" she said exultantly, throwing her arms around Ty's neck. "That's the best thing anyone's ever done for me."

"Just taking you flying? That's too bad." He kissed her fingertips. "You deserve more."

"No one could give me more than you just did." Sun, moon and stars, it was everything she'd dreamed of. "We flew with the birds." Her laugh held pure joy. "You're wonderful. I love it. I love—" she stopped, suddenly afraid of what she was going to say next. It was as though thousand-watt stadium lighting had just come on, showing her what had been there all along.

Showing her that while she'd been so smugly congratulating herself on keeping her heart to herself, it had long since been firmly his.

15

TY SAT in his studio, prepping one of the paper collages he used for canvases. He meticulously folded sheets into small squares, then nailed each into place on the backing board. Once he'd covered it with gesso, he'd project on his base a level photographic image, and then he'd come in with paint.

He glanced up and found Trish staring at him from the door to his studio. She jumped guiltily.

"Hey," he said. "No fair standing so far away. Come on over."

"I have to go hit the grocery and the art supply store," she said. "Did you need anything besides what's on your list?"

He considered. "Eternal adoration?"

She gave a shaky laugh. "I don't know that that's covered in your contract." Her smile vanished too quickly.

Ty studied her. "Are you okay?"

"Yeah, sure. Why shouldn't I be?"

It was a good question and one he couldn't answer. He remembered soaring with her, the exuberant expression on her face when they'd landed. But somehow, on

the way home, things had turned awkward. She'd re-
treated into silence, and that night she'd gone home to
her own house. She'd made excuses about making
changes to her script, but it was clear that she wanted
to be alone.

Stop letting it get to you, he told himself. *Leave it
alone.* Backing off made sense, anyway. It had always
been his M.O., at least before Trish. Maybe it had all
just gotten too intense too quickly. Maybe what she
wanted was to ease off the one-on-one time.

"I was thinking we could go out to dinner somewhere tonight for a change," he said casually. "Get out
of the house."

Trish's shoulders tightened. "I thought I'd go home
tonight," she said.

He suppressed the urge to remind her of the night before. "How about after?" he said, even as he told himself to let it go.

"Well, no, I…"

Watching her flounder gave him no comfort at all.
"Some other time, then," he said briefly, trying to push
away the frustration. "Did you get the script copied?"

"I did." She hesitated. "Are you sure you want to
show it to people? I mean, I don't want you doing it just
to help me out."

"You already said that and I told you, I want Michael." He came to press a kiss on her and pulled her
against him. For an instant, she softened. "Relax, it's
not like I'm going to expect you to put out if we make
your movie."

A week before, she'd have given a bawdy response,

like as not. Instead, she just sighed, but held on to him as though he were a lifeline.

"Trish," Ty said softly. "You know I care about you, right?" *Don't push it.* He bit back the words that had come too easily to him in the past.

Trish didn't say anything for a moment, then raised her head and looked at him. "And I care about you." She brushed her mouth against his.

He couldn't keep himself from taking it deeper, into warmth and softness. He'd never considered himself a needy person, and suddenly he felt as though he was trying to hold water in his fists. He ended the kiss, even though he thirsted for more. "Okay." He slapped her on the behind. "Drive safely."

But his eyes, when he sat down at his worktable, were troubled.

TRISH STOOD in the art supply store staring at the tubes of acrylic paints. Funny how everyone always associated colors with emotions. Seeing red, pea green with envy, black-hearted, blue. There wasn't a color for the roiling nerves she felt. There wasn't a color for feeling as though she was a crash-test dummy just seconds from getting slammed into a wall. How in God's name could she have let herself fall in love with Ty Ramsay?

How could she have thought for a moment that she wouldn't?

All the days and nights she'd told herself she had it handled, as though knowing her heart was going to be broken was enough. Had there ever really been a point when she could have walked away unscathed, she wondered, or had she just been lying to herself the whole time?

Now, all she could feel was panicked. It was going to end; she'd always known it was going to end.

The difference was, now it was actually happening.

TY PROJECTED the picture of Trish's face onto the canvas and stared at it as though looking would help him understand what she needed, what she wanted. What was it beneath the elusive loveliness? What was the answer to the riddle of Trish?

The tone sounded that indicated someone was driving through the front gate. Too soon for Trish to be back, he reminded himself, but he was already making plans. It was time to talk, really talk. He'd tell her how he felt, not settle for doing it halfway.

This time, he'd do it.

It wasn't Trish's silver Hyundai he saw when he looked out the front window, though, but Charlie's red Prius.

Ty leaned against the front doorjamb and watched his friend approach.

"What brings you out here?"

"I was visiting a buddy up the canyon. Thought I'd stop in and see if you were out of rehearsals yet."

"Finished last week. We start shooting interiors Monday." A solid month of dawn-to-dusk filming, foregoing daylight to immerse himself in a fantasy world. And after that, night shoots on the streets of L.A., swapping his schedule for that of a vampire.

Thanks to Trish's work, it was the most nuanced

role he'd had to date. Why then did he catch himself focusing on the script he wished he were shooting? Why was it he just kept brooding?

Charlie ambled up onto the porch, a satchel slung over his shoulder. "Got any coffee, *compadre?*"

Ty grinned. *"Mi java es su java."*

"Gracias, amigo." He followed Ty into the kitchen. "So how's *Dark Touch* doing? You weren't too thrilled last time we talked."

Ty poured coffee into a mug and handed it to him. "It's all taken care of now."

Charlie sniffed appreciatively and took a sip. "What happened with the script. Did they bring in another writer?"

"Yeah, as a matter of fact." Ty poured a cup for himself.

"Who?"

"My new assistant, Trish."

Charlie started to take another drink, then lowered his mug. "Trish? Wasn't that the name of the woman you met a couple of weeks ago?"

"Yeah, so?"

"Didn't realize you'd promoted her," Charlie said slowly. "How'd she get involved with *Dark Touch,* anyway? You didn't pull one of those high-maintenance star things, did you? Because as a director and your friend I'd have to slap you upside the head."

"Relax, it didn't play that way. She was working on some office stuff here and we got walking through the script and she just started coming through with this great material."

"Dale's letting some amateur from nowhere rewrite his script?" Charlie asked skeptically. "Or is there something I don't know and she's a guild member?"

"Jeez, you'd think you were a guild member yourself." The snap of annoyance was quick and sharp. "No, Dale's not having Trish do a rewrite. I showed him the first set of lines and he liked them, which wasn't hard because the old dialog sucked wind. She did more and he liked that, too. She's just focusing on the trouble spots, adding a little English to the characters in a couple of places. It's not a rewrite."

Charlie let a little chuckle escape.

"What?" Ty asked.

Charlie shook his head. "Nothing. Let's go out on the deck."

Ty slid the screen door closed behind them and dropped down into one of the Adirondack chairs. The warm spell was continuing, and his short-sleeved cotton shirt felt right. "So, to what do I owe this honor, besides your buddy up the canyon?"

Charlie sat down next to him. "I figured I'd swing by and see how the meeting with Tate went. That was yesterday, right?"

"Yeah. All my Mondays should start so well. He says we should get a couple of projects together and set up a meeting with him."

"Underwriter?"

Ty shook his head. "He's not about to do full funding—made lots of references to my asking price—but I think we could get him to come up with a chunk of it."

"Chunks work for me," Charlie said, "I'll take chunks."

"You want chunks, we need scripts."

Charlie considered. "I've got that script I told you about. It's good. Most of the other stuff I've been looking at in the past coupla' days is mediocre, at best. The optioned one is a cut above, though. *Memoirs of a Geisha* meets Elmore Leonard."

"You're joking."

"Actually, yes. It's an adaptation of *The Piano Tuner.* In fact, I just so happen to have it here." He pulled it out of his satchel.

"Well, do tell. How about that for a coincidence?"

Charlie smiled broadly. "How about."

"Well, don't worry about the second script. I've actually stumbled across a property that's good, really good," Ty said.

"Oh, yeah?" Charlie sat up. "Give me a rundown."

"Small, sensitive film, sort of *Party of Five* meets *Mystic River* meets John Gotti. South Boston. Older sister raises sibs, and when she's ready to get a life finds romance with a neighborhood guy."

"And the Gotti part?"

"Neighborhood guy has skirted the edge of the law and his brother is a mobster who's a fugitive from the FBI. Maybe the neighborhood guy's covering up for little brother and maybe he's not. It's not played for the crime-suspense part, though, it's more a character study. Heroine's got trust and confidence issues and finds out first time out of the gate that her heartthrob is maybe a bad guy. Meanwhile, he's got to choose between family and love, because he really does love this woman."

Charlie looked at him with interest. "And would the neighborhood guy be played by anyone I know?"

"Triumph the Insult Comic Dog."

"My guess."

"It's a good script, Charlie," Ty said, all joking gone. "It's a movie we should make. Take a look at it."

Charlie studied him. "So who wrote it?"

"Someone cheap."

"And that would be?"

"What does it matter?"

"Call it intuition. Who is it?" Charlie asked, more insistent now.

Ty let out a breath. "Trish."

"Trish." Charlie nodded, pursing his lips. "You mean your new assistant, Trish."

"Yeah. It's a good script, maybe even great," Ty added, thinking of the last version he'd read.

"Great, huh? This is getting better all the time. And her rewrites on *Dark Touch* are great, too."

Ty's jaw tightened. "You didn't see the original version. Dale wouldn't have bought into her changes if he hadn't agreed."

"He wouldn't, say, do it to keep his high-priced box-office stud happy, right?"

"Nobody asked him to." An edge entered Ty's voice. "All I did was show it to him and he decided the rest. Dale doesn't put himself out to suck up to people. If he says something's good, it's because it is."

Charlie was shaking his head. "Man, you are nothing if not predictable."

"What's that supposed to mean?"

"What, I've got to spell it out for you? I mean, Christ, how many times do you have to go through this? You're working with her, you fall for her. You fall for her, you want to make her world perfect for when you're gone by setting her up in business. Rinse and repeat."

Ty's expression hardened. "The only reason you're still sitting there is because we go back too far for me to punch you."

"Save your energy and punch yourself. Maybe it'll knock some sense into you. Can you honestly tell me that falling for someone you're working on a script with is that much different than falling for your costar?"

"This is totally different. And what's it your business, anyway?"

"What's it..." Charlie slammed down his fist. "If you saw me drunk and trying to get into a car and drive, would you try to stop me? I was around for rounds one, two and three, remember? The parts where you were feeling like crap, remember those?" He subsided. "Just tell me you haven't proposed to her yet. She hasn't started picking out china patterns so you'll have stuff to throw at each other, has she?"

"No." The day's misgivings suddenly took shape. "I think she's getting ready to bail."

Charlie looked at him more closely. "Really? Is that what optioning this script is all about?"

"No," Ty blazed. "The script stands on its own. Dammit, just read it, you'll see."

"But getting the script made into a movie doesn't hurt, right?"

"Hell, I don't know." Frustration clawed at him. "She's the most amazing woman I've ever known, and the most guarded. I mean, she's smart, sexy, funny, talented. I can talk with her, you know? And yet I can't get her to open up, I can't get her to trust me."

"You got to admit, your track record doesn't inspire a whole lot of confidence. Maybe that's it."

"Maybe. There's some stuff I know about from her past, but it's like she's held on to it, instead of working through it. And I'm trying to understand, but there's a point where I start wondering if I'm not just being a putz by hanging around and hoping that she'll let me in." He lapsed into silence, staring moodily out at the canyon.

"Well, I've got to hand it to you," Charlie said conversationally. "Every other relationship you've been in, you've never stuck when the going got tough. When the make-believe ended, you were always gone."

"Thank you, Doctor."

Charlie shook his head. "You're missing my point. It sounds like you're actually trying to work with this one. I don't know if it'll get you anywhere, but you're at least trying to move in the right direction."

"Whatever that is." And how could they go anywhere when Trish was dead set against it? Ty leaned back in his chair and looked up at the sky. "I mean, I thought we were getting somewhere a couple of days ago, I really did. I took her gliding and you should have seen her face. It was like she'd found God or something. But now all of a sudden she's acting like she's got one foot out the door again."

"One foot out the door how?"

"Distant. Won't meet my eyes."

"She seeing someone else?"

Ty shook his head. Whatever was between them, it wasn't another man. "She hasn't had the chance. I'm not sure, maybe I just need to wait her out. But she keeps pulling back. I don't think she would play me, but then I wonder. And it makes me fell like a sucker."

"Yeah."

"It could be that waiting's not going to do it," he said, finally facing his biggest fear. "It could be that this is just how she is and I'm getting caught up in the idea that I can fix it and fix her. Maybe I can't. Maybe she's not fixable. I shouldn't even want to. You said it yourself, I don't hang around when the going gets tough. Next thing you know, maybe I'm sick of it all, I'm sick of her, and I just want it over."

There was a noise from within the house. Ty whipped his head around to see the outline of a figure through the screen.

Trish.

"Shit." He vaulted to his feet and yanked open the screen. "Trish?"

The front door was flung open and in a flash of sunlight, she vaulted through it.

Toward her car.

"Trish!" He ran across the parking apron. "Where are you going?"

She turned at her car door to face him. "Gee, I don't know. How about anywhere that's not here?" Her face was pale, except where two spots of color flashed on her cheeks.

"What did you hear?"

"All I needed to. Just a little chat with your buddy, huh?"

"You and I are the ones who should be talking."

"And I think we've done all the talking we need to," she retorted, glaring at him. "You know, if you wanted all of this over, Ty, all you had to do was say it. You want me gone, I'm gone."

"I don't want you gone."

"It sure sounded like it to me." For the first time, her voice shook. "I've got to hand it to you, you move fast. From 'this means something to me' to 'I'm sick of her.' Forget about zero to sixty in three seconds, you go sixty to zero twice as fast." She dug in her purse for her keys.

"That wasn't what I was saying, you heard it wrong."

"My hearing was fine last time I got it checked." She snapped, fumbling to get the key into the lock.

"Trish. Look at me," his voice softened, "I care about you."

She turned to face him again. "Pardon me if I'm not convinced."

"Don't go carting off because you caught something I said out of context."

She gave a choking laugh and leaned against the car, crossing her arms over her chest. "Oh, this is good. So what, exactly, was the context?"

Now his own frustration billowed up. "That I don't know what we're doing here. It's two steps forward and two steps back with you. I keep trying and trying, but

I don't know what it takes. And after a while I start wondering if there's a point."

"Besides, you're starting a new movie. Time for a change of scenery, isn't it?" The tip of her nose pinkened.

"No, it's not."

"Yes, it is," she returned, blinking furiously. "I'd be out of my mind to let myself really care about you, Ty. I know about you, you don't do long-term." She opened the car door and slipped into her seat. "Well, neither do I."

"Sure, why get involved?" Anger coursed through him unchecked. "After all, if you did that you'd have to take a risk, and you can't do that when you're running. It slows you down."

"When did you become such an expert?"

He thought he saw the shimmer of tears in her eyes and his anger died. "Don't go, Trish." His words came gently. "This isn't the time to run."

"Oh, no," she said, turning the key in the ignition. "The time for that was the first time I met you."

SHE DROVE TOO FAST and a little recklessly down the winding canyon road, the tears, finally, slipping down her cheeks. She'd known, she'd always known it wasn't going to last. She'd thought she was being smart.

She never thought she'd fall in love with him.

She reached the intersection with Pacific Coast Highway, but home was the last place she wanted to go. She didn't want to cry for him in her stifling little apartment. She didn't want to be in the city at all. Instead, she turned right. The road ahead of her blurred a bit and she blinked as she passed the hummock of rock, watching for the turnout.

And there, finally, she laid her head against the steering wheel and wept.

How, after all the years, had she put herself in the same spot again? The betrayal by someone she loved, someone she thought cared for her. She'd always known it would end, but she'd expected to find out in a conversation between adults, not by overhearing a brutally offhand dissection. Open up, he'd said, and she'd told him some of what had formed her. And he'd understood so little of what she'd told him that he'd casually done the exact same thing. It had been day rather than night, they'd been drinking coffee rather than beer, but the words had been the same, the sickening feeling of humiliation and worthlessness had been the same.

She lifted her head slowly. Or had it been the same? Before the tears had come anger. Something creaked inside her, like some floodgate long rusted shut. She wasn't worthless, she knew that deep down. The difficult part had always been believing it. Yes, right now it felt as if a hole had been carved in her, but she would get past it and go forward. She would. And eventually Ty Ramsay wouldn't matter anymore.

Maybe nothing would.

16

"HAVE YOU ever felt ice so cold it was hot?" Ty asked, his fingers framing Caitlyn's face as he leaned over her on the couch. His voice was silky, his gaze intent.

She stared back at him in a thrall of arousal.

"That's what it's about," he said softly, "the point where the senses break down, the point where… where…" Ty stopped in midline, and cursed, his mind suddenly blank.

"Cut!" Dale called.

Ty shook his head. "Sorry. I just lost track there."

Caitlyn still watched him with eyes that were slumberous and dark.

"That was our twelfth take," Dale reminded him. "You need to get it together."

Ty blew out an impatient breath. "I know. Give me five minutes and I'll nail it."

"All right, but stop by makeup before you come back," he directed. "You look tired."

Not sleeping did that to a person, Ty thought as he sat in the chair, ignoring the makeup girl's chatter. It was hard to know what was worse, lying in an empty bed and staring at the ceiling or waking in the morning and reaching for Trish in that first split second of consciousness.

Only to realize she wasn't there.

The days weren't so bad. Work gave him a place to go, a chance to put his mind on hold while he became somebody else. The problem was, thoughts of her kept intruding even there. What was the point? he asked himself. They weren't living out *Wuthering Heights,* it wasn't a foolish misunderstanding that had broken them up, it was real issues, trust, openness. And it wasn't just Trish's lack of trust in him. If he were honest, he'd lacked trust in himself. At some level, maybe he'd felt free to care for Trish precisely because she was always ready to run. That didn't mean he was happy now. Far from it.

He couldn't remember feeling anything after his previous breakups except relief and guilt, but then again he'd usually distracted himself immediately with women and work. There was nothing like a tough action role for losing yourself.

Except that it wasn't working this time around.

In the makeup chair next to him, Caitlyn gave him a leisurely survey. "You're looking a little worse for the wear, there." As her confidence had grown in the weeks they'd worked together, so had her interest.

"Worrying about keeping up with you is keeping me up at night."

"I know some good ways to help you sleep." Her smile was warm with invitation.

There was a time he would have taken her up on it

without a thought. Now, he responded just as automatically. "I'll survive," he said lightly. "Thanks for the offer."

TRISH WALKED THROUGH the lobby of Amber's Assistants. She barely glanced at Laurel, who was pushing back her cuticles and reading a book on the South Beach Diet. The familiar twinge of annoyance didn't hit; then again she hadn't been real good at feeling much of anything in the past several days except gnawing loss. It would get better, she told herself. She just needed to wait it out.

And in ten or twenty years, she'd be right as rain.

"Nice of you to stop in," Amber said as Trish walked into her office.

"You wanted to see me?"

"If I want to see you, all I have to do is look in the press." Amber slapped down an entertainment magazine open to the gossip page. And there, in living color, was a photo of Ty at the gallery, with a laughing Trish encircled by the curve of his arm.

It took the breath from her lungs. She wouldn't react, Trish told herself fiercely. She wouldn't remember that night and she wouldn't, she absolutely couldn't cry. Looking away was equally impossible, though. It pulled her back in time, to the way it had felt to be with him, to the feeling of seeing his smile from across the room and knowing it was for her and her alone.

And all she could think was that she couldn't bear it.

"This is totally unacceptable, Trish." Amber's voice

dragged her back to the present. "Even for you this is below par. As the company head, I'm humiliated to see this picture. Think how it looks to clients or future clients."

"Amber, I didn't plan it," Trish said wearily, "it just happened."

"Nothing can 'just happen' when you're an assistant," Amber snapped. "You start maintaining a respectful distance from the client. I don't care if nothing happened, the papers are reporting it as though something did."

Trish blinked. Amber always had been good at seeing only what she wanted to. It would never in a million years occur to her that the article might actually have been true. Trish as someone who might have a lover didn't fit into her world view. Or was she just jealous?

"I don't particularly care for what you wore, although it's a cut above your usual. From now on, if you're going to be at a public function, I want you to look professional. Suits only, and I want you to do something about your hair. I won't have you making Amber's Assistants look bad."

There was a roaring in Trish's ears. It was all about Amber, always all about Amber, salted with regular asides on Trish's many failings. For how many years had that been all she'd heard? For how many years had the echoes bounced around her own head? The occasional laughter and good times didn't make up for it by half. And suddenly, as Trish stared at the photo of herself with Ty, it all crystallized.

"I quit," she said suddenly, cutting Amber off in midstream.

Amber blinked. "What did you say?"

"I quit. Sayonara, enough. You've got two weeks' notice, if you want, but I'm off the Ramsay job effective right now."

"You can't quit," Amber spluttered. "I won't have it."

"Nevertheless," Trish said calmly.

"But the Ramsay contract's the most important one I've got."

"Call him," Trish suggested. "I'm sure you can persuade him."

Amber's eyes narrowed. "Is this about Laurel's raise?"

"Laurel's raise?" Faint surprise and contempt were all she was able to muster up. "How nice for her."

"I can look at the books," Amber said grudgingly. "It might not hurt to bump you up a bit."

"Amber," Trish said gently, "I'm quitting. Period."

Amber's face reddened. "Oh, sure, go ahead and leave me high and dry, after spending time job-hunting on my nickel."

"No, actually. There isn't a new job. I'm just realizing that this isn't working for either of us."

"It's working for me."

And that pretty much said it all. Trish took a deep breath. "Okay, let me be clear about this. This is not working for me. It hasn't for a long time. It's best for me to move on." Habit and the sudden, desperate look on Amber's face gave Trish the immediate urge to fix things so that her sister was okay. She couldn't do it all, though.

Finally, she'd realized that. It was time she stood up for herself.

"But…I want things to stay like they were," Amber said, as if saying the words would make it so.

This was real life, though. Nothing stayed the same, Trish thought, staring at the photo of Ty. Nothing at all.

THE KNOCK CAME on Ty's trailer door. "On the set, Mr. Ramsay."

He looked up from the script he'd been reading, or rather staring at, for the past several minutes. He was supposed to be reviewing his lines, putting on the mantle of his role. It had always been easy for him to inhabit the exaggerated reality of a character living larger-than-life events and emotions. What had been harder was settling for the nuances of everyday life.

He'd grown up with parents who'd met and married after just two weeks to start a life-long love affair. Their explanation had always been that they just knew. Ty had grown up expecting grand emotions. He'd thought that was what life was all about.

And in film, he thought, walking out of his trailer and onto the set, it was. More than anything, that had been why he'd leaped into relationship after relationship that had started with a roar and ended in a whimper. On the set, everything felt immediate and real. The connection with the woman acting opposite him was always tangible and absorbing. How easy it had been to confuse those feelings with the romance of his parents' story. In the heat of filming, Ty had always been convinced that this was the one.

The problem was, filming eventually stopped.

He sat in the makeup chair for a last brushup, nodding to Caitlyn and trying to evade her come-on gaze. That wasn't the tone they needed now. This was the scene in which his character dealt with the aftermath of finding a murderer in his inner circle, dealt with the betrayal of learning that the woman he loved had been lying about who she was, to him, to everyone. That, despite the flash and intimacy of their connection, she'd blocked him out.

And now she was gone.

"Places, everyone."

Ty walked over to sit behind the heavy walnut desk in what was his character's Edwardian office. The continuity girl leaned in to adjust his collar.

The thing to do was to take on that betrayal, that frustration, that loss, and channel it into his performance. To make himself go through it and then give it to his character. It would be easy, he thought.

It was what he was feeling already about Trish.

The thought hit him with the impact of a punch. The emotions his character was facing were nothing compared to what he'd been through over the past two weeks. Filming could stop right now and he'd still be feeling them, because they were real. This wasn't about life imitating art, this was about his art imitating his life.

And that quickly, he knew what he wanted, no matter what it took. This wasn't where things stopped for Trish and him, it couldn't be. Their love story wasn't finished, it had scenes and scenes ahead. They just needed to revise it, to fix the dialog, adjust the character motivations.

And find their future, together.

"Everybody ready?" Dale said. "Rolling, and…action."

And Ty began to turn life into art.

"BOY, YOU HAD THAT ONE on the first take, Ty. I've never seen anything like it." Dale slapped him on the shoulder as they stood in the twilight outside the sound stage. "I took a look at the rushes during lunch and that's the one I'm going to use."

Now Dale told him, Ty thought, remembering the hours of retakes, reaction shots, and cutaways he'd endured when all he'd wanted to do was go find Trish. Because Ty was a professional, he'd stifled his impatience and given each take maximum effort. It hadn't been difficult. All the feeling was there waiting to be tapped, including the exhilaration at the end when Caitlyn's character comes back to him.

The way he hoped Trish would come back. And now, all he wanted was to be gone.

"Glad you're happy, Dale. I'm going to get cleaned up and head out."

"Have a great weekend." Dale gave him an affable smile. "Don't forget, the night shoot starts Monday, up on Fairfax. It's on your production sheet."

"I'll be there."

But he had other places to be first.

TRISH TURNED OFF Fairfax on to Sixth Street and headed toward the entrance of Park La Brea. In the dusk, the cars behind her were mostly glaring headlights that dazzled her eyes. Just more commuters heading home. She swung into the gate area and waited for it to open, not looking, particularly, at the car that got into line behind her.

Of course, lately she hadn't been able to focus on much of anything. It was lucky that the temp job she'd landed required little more than consciousness. If it didn't pay particularly well, at least it didn't demand much from her.

Then again, it did nothing to distract her from thinking about Ty. It would get easier, she told herself automatically. That had become her mantra. She'd get past it the same way she'd finally gotten past Amber, and she'd be okay.

She *was* okay. Deep inside her, something shifted, that rusty gate opening just a millimeter. Her time with Ty represented just another of the experiences that had brought her to this point, she reminded herself.

Trish chose a parking spot absently, mentally tabulating her list of job-search tasks to do that night. Turning off the car, she groped for her bag. She needed to get a dozen résumés ready to go out that night. The economy was picking up; she might be able to find something in PR, she thought as she got out of her car. Of course, jobs made her think of her script, and her script made her think of Ty, which she hadn't done in, oh, thirty seconds. A new record.

She wondered when it would stop, this swamping gloom that rolled over her every time he came to mind. She wondered when she'd stop wishing for the impossible, wondering how it could have turned out differently.

She wondered when she'd stop loving him.

And then she looked up and saw him standing at the nose of her car.

THE SKY WAS DEEPENING to purple. The parking lot lights switched on, bathing the area in the bluish tones of fluorescence. Another commuter slammed his car door shut and headed to his apartment. Trish stood frozen, looking at Ty.

He'd conjured her face up again and again in the nearly two weeks since he'd seen her last. The lips he'd seen curve so many times in pleasure were now parted in shock.

Moments later, though, she unfroze, but the freeze was on in another way. Their initial eye contact had crackled with connection. Now, he saw, her eyes had chilled. Now, the walls were in place.

"Hey, you," he said.

She shrugged by way of answer. "What are you doing here?" The weather had turned cool again and the brisk wind made her shiver a little in her pea coat.

"I was hoping to talk with you for a little. Can we go inside?"

It took her a minute to decide. "Not long," she said finally. "I've got dinner plans."

"It'll be quick," he promised, trying not to wonder who those plans might involve.

They walked through the courtyard. "Amber told me you'd quit," he said. And the news had given him hope. If she'd found the strength to stand up to her sister, what else might have changed? "I think it was a good move for you."

Trish threw him a surprised glance, then looked away. "It was time," was all she said.

In her apartment, she rapidly flipped on all the lights, as though to banish any possible intimacy. Ty sat on the couch. There was room beside him; instead, she chose the chair.

And waited.

People always joked that actors couldn't talk outside of films because there weren't any lines written down for them. Ty had never had a problem with it. Now, though, he found himself tongue-tied. There was so much he wanted to tell her, but he didn't know how to get it across, how to make her believe it.

How to make her believe in herself.

Her stiff posture warned him to keep his distance. Her face was thinner; lines of strain made it clear that the past two weeks hadn't been any easier for her than for him. What they didn't tell him was how she felt about his being there.

He took a deep breath. "We never finished our talk the other day."

"I thought we said everything that needed to be said."

He couldn't read her expression. Nerves, certainly, and wariness. "I don't think we said nearly enough. I thought maybe now we've both cooled off, we could try again." He swallowed. "I know I hurt you."

"I'm fine," she said quickly, but he heard the ache beneath her words and knew she lied. She wasn't fine any more than he was.

Guilt twisted at him. "I didn't plan to have it happen that way."

Trish squeezed her eyes shut briefly, the way a person would at a body blow. "Just how exactly did you plan it to happen?"

"I didn't plan for anything. I told you before, Trish, I care about you." He stopped, impatient with himself. "Look, I know I don't have the best record around. It's just that when you're in a movie with someone, you get caught up in the role. You've got the lighting, the costumes, the set, everything telling you that you should be falling for that person. You spend day after day convincing yourself that the emotions you're making yourself feel are real."

"Is this the part where you tell me about Caitlyn?" she asked, her voice barely audible.

"That's not…I'm screwing this up," he muttered. Without thinking, he reached for her hand, but she shifted away.

"No," she said sharply, her voice stronger now. "Finish what you came here to say."

Everything that had seemed so straightforward that afternoon was now lost in the maze of his thoughts. All he knew was that he needed her, but he had to tell her why. He had to make her understand that she wasn't just another in a line. He had to make her trust.

Ty blew out a breath and tried again. "This whole thing with my costars, it was because I mixed up fantasy and reality."

"The way we did working on your script."

"No. What was between us was real. Is real," he amended. "It's not because of the script."

"How do you know? Can you honestly say you didn't get caught up in it? I did." She blinked a little and he felt his heart clutch.

"Yes, I got caught up in it, but that wasn't all. You mean something to me, Trish."

"Do I really, or is it tangled up with play-acting?" she challenged. "*Dark Touch,* bondage…you even brought my script into it. Was that real, or was that just something to make me feel good?"

It was a lead line out of the maze and all he could think about was grabbing it. "It wasn't just to make you feel good and you should know that." He rounded on her. "Michael is my role, and my partner Charlie is foaming at the mouth to direct the whole thing."

Trish shook her head in confusion. "Wait a minute. I thought you were just going to show the script around. Now you're talking about actually filming? You told me you had a whole lineup of projects."

"Yours was the right one." Confidence buoyed him. It was a way out of his action-hero box, and it was a way to tie them together. It was right. "We have an outside investor coming in with a quarter of the budget. If you're ready to sell the option, we're ready to go."

"And the rest of the money, where does that come from?" Trish asked carefully.

"Me." He'd expected excitement. Earlier in the day, he'd imagined their celebration. A celebration of the two of them, for the two of them. Instead, they seemed further apart than ever. And he watched the light die out in her eyes. "I thought it would be good news," he said quietly.

"I don't know about good." Her voice was brittle. "It's certainly tidy."

"What's tidy?"

She tilted her head. "Oh, Jocasta gets a gallery, I get a script greenlit, Megan gets…well, I don't know what Megan got, but I'm sure it was something nice. You're very good to the women you sleep with. I don't know if you're coming after me to get to the script or if you're coming after the script to get to me. Do you?"

"This isn't about manipulation," he countered. "I want this role, plain and simple. What's between you and me has nothing to do with that."

"Prove it," she demanded. "You want the script, then let's do the script. Period."

Ty blinked. "And walk away from this?"

"You can't have it both ways, Ty. Don't you see?" Her voice trembled. "You talk about figuring out how you mix things up, but you've mixed us up, too. Between our working together and the script and whatever was between you and me, you've mixed it around until none of it's real."

"It is real," he said heatedly, "you just won't trust it."

"And why should I trust it?" Her voice rose. "I remember hearing you and Charlie talk. Why should I believe what you say?"

"Because I love you."

His whispered words hung in the air. Trish caught her breath for a moment and then her eyes flashed. "It's not that easy, Ty. You can't just throw out the words and expect them to fix things." She shot to her feet. "You want me to believe, to trust? Then give me a reason to."

He stood. "What do you want then? Do you want me to get out of the loop, leave it all up to Charlie?"

"Yes."

"And what about us?"

"What us? You want this script, then we do the script. And when that's done, if whatever you imagine you feel for me hasn't evaporated, we'll deal with that."

He walked to the door and turned. "It's not going to evaporate, Trish."

"I wish I had your faith," she said softly.

He gave her a humorless smile. "Looks like I'll have to have enough faith for both of us."

17

IT WAS EXTRAORDINARY how quickly life could change, Trish thought as she looked down the table at Rebecca's to see the rest of the Supper Club. Two months before, when they'd all been at Sabrina's party, she'd been walking dogs and grocery shopping for a living. Now she was script-doctoring, fielding calls from an agent, and planning for the first preproduction meeting on her own screenplay. She'd taken a huge step toward self-liberation and a step toward living out her dreams.

If only she could feel it.

No one's life came together like a fairy tale, she reminded herself. So she still had to temp occasionally to pay the bills. So Amber had yet to speak to her since her resignation.

So she still woke in the mornings longing for Ty.

Her life was still a work in progress, but progress it was.

As though she'd heard Trish's thoughts, Delaney raised her glass. "All right, now that we've finished toasting Sabrina and Stef and romantic engagements on Santorini, here's to Trish and her emancipation from slavery," she proclaimed. "I only wish you'd been able to get a videotape of Amber's face when you did it," she added to Trish.

"Don't remind me," Trish said ruefully. "I still get the guilts over it."

"Don't." Cilla's voice was emphatic. "It was the best thing you've ever done, finally standing up for yourself." She signed the charge slip for the meal and handed the black folder back to the waiter.

"It's huge, you know," Thea agreed. "You're different. I mean, something's changed in you. Something changed in order for you to be able to do it and doing it changed something in you."

"You're so hot when you talk like a psychiatrist, Thea," Sabrina said playfully.

It was true, though, Trish thought. Day by day, that rusty little part inside her, the part that let her believe in herself, creaked open a little more.

"Laugh all you want, Cilla," Thea threw back, "but you watch. Things are going to change with her."

Cilla laughed. "I think things are changing with you, Thea. That's the first time I've seen you wear something besides black since you moved back from New York. What is that, charcoal?"

"Oh, you complain, but you love it," Thea retorted, glancing at Cilla's op-art print shirt. "It makes me the perfect foil for you."

"If I had your bone structure, I could get away with wearing black and skinning my hair back, too." Cilla sighed.

Thea gave her a judicious look. "You wouldn't, though. You love being the peacock too much."

"Ain't it the truth," Cilla grinned. "So, is our work here done?"

The group rose from the table and began straggling toward the door. Cilla held back to talk with Trish. "How are you doing?" she asked quietly.·

Trish sighed. "Okay, I guess. Trying not to think too much. Work helps."

"Have you heard from Ty?"

"No. He's keeping his word so far. He hasn't been involved in any of the initial contract talks."

"So is that good or bad?"

Trish gave a laugh that ended in a choke. "I'll let you know when I figure it out."

"He's not the only man who's ever going to be interested in you," Cilla reminded her. "I mean, look how the waiter was flirting with you tonight."

But the waiter didn't make her feel the way Ty had. She wasn't sure anyone else ever would. Out at the curb, she glanced over to see Sabrina waiting in line for the valet. "Listen, I've got to go," she said quickly.

Cilla saw the direction of her gaze and nodded. "Yeah, you do. Good luck." She gave Trish a quick hug. "Don't worry, it'll go fine."

Trish walked up to where Sabrina waited for her car. "Hey."

Sabrina turned, her eyes bright with fun. "So can I tell you how much I love being where I can eavesdrop on people and actually understand what they're saying again? Although I was actually starting to pick up some Greek toward the end," she reflected.

"You might need to go back to the islands for another few months to get fluent, huh?"

"Maybe on our honeymoon," she agreed, the sapphire on her finger flashing under the lights.

Where to start, Trish thought. "There's something I need to tell you." *You know the cousin you told us all to avoid? Well I slept with him.* Or maybe, *I'm actually a closet groupie, so I did your cousin.* Stop stalling and do it, she told herself. "I don't know how you'll take this but I just had an affair with your cousin."

Sabrina blinked. *"Lee?"*

Trish started to laugh and ended up coughing. "No, your other cousin."

"Ty?" Shock spread over her features. "But how?"

Trish shrugged. "We met at your party. He hired me to work for him."

Sabrina clutched at her arm. "Oh God, Trish, what did he do? I'm so sorry."

"Relax, he didn't do anything." *Except steal my heart,* she thought. "Anyway, I'm the one who should be sorry."

"Why?"

"Poaching on your family."

Sabrina snorted. "Ty's a big boy. He can take care of himself. Although he did promise to stop going after my friends," she reflected. "Actually, he swore to me that he was off dating and sleeping around or I never would have even invited him that night. We all wondered where you disappeared to. Why didn't you tell us? You were being kind of cagey about the script stuff, now that I think about it."

Trish winced. "I was embarrassed. I mean, you'd warned us all. Besides, he's so far out of my league it would have sounded like a joke."

"What's that supposed to mean?" Sabrina asked with an edge to her voice. "He was lucky to have you."

"It still wasn't smart. I'm not sorry I did it, but I can see how it would have looked to you guys."

"Oh, come on, you know how it goes. Advice, yeah, but you've got to let your friends live their lives, and you stay around to pick up the pieces if they need you to."

Trish hugged her and felt the sting of tears.

"So tell me he wasn't a complete nightmare at the end. Tell me he broke it off nicely," Sabrina said, automatically taking the keys the valet handed her.

"Well…"

"Or at least semihumanely. What did he say?"

"Well…" Trish said awkwardly "…he told me he loved me."

Sabrina made an impatient noise. "God, what a jerk. The old 'I love you but…'"

"No," Trish said in a small voice, "just 'I love you.'"

A beat went by. "So you're still having an affair, then. The way you sounded, it was over."

"It is. More or less."

Sabrina blinked and handed her keys back to the valet. "Sorry, we're going back inside," she said. "I've got to hear this whole thing from the beginning."

TRISH STOOD in front of her full-length mirror and gave herself a final check. True, she wasn't as skilled as

Cilla at doing blow-outs, but she'd done a respectable job, she thought, shaking her mostly smooth hair. Good enough for a meeting, anyway. It wasn't as though she was trying out for a role, it was just a preproduction meeting on her script.

The forest-green pantsuit was a holdover from her PR days, with its short, tailored jacket and smooth trousers. It brought out her eyes and made her skin look luminous, though it hung on her more than a bit, now that she looked at it critically. She'd lost ten pounds over the previous month that showed everywhere. Time to get an appetite again, she told herself, though it was hard to care.

Of course, if she could work instant miracles on her appearance she'd probably get rid of the dark circles that persisted under her eyes. Even today's cosmetics couldn't make them disappear entirely. It wasn't that sleep eluded her, but it was rarely restful. Thea could probably have lectured her about the anxiety dreams that dogged her. Maybe they were driven by the pressures that came with her screenwriting projects, and maybe they were manifestations of guilt over Amber.

And maybe they were just a manifestation of missing Ty.

Trish shook her head and left the bedroom. It wasn't as if they were going to refuse to work her script because her suit didn't fit. There was no reason to be nervous; her new agent would be there to ensure all went well. It was just a meeting with the producer and the director to discuss her responsibilities. And just because the producer happened to be Ty didn't mean she'd fall apart.

She'd be fine.

She repeated it to herself over and over on the drive to the office space that was GDI Films. She repeated it as she parked, as she sat in the lobby and even when the receptionist showed her to the conference room.

"Trish!" Roberta Van Dorn might have looked and sounded like a debutante, but she was as tough as they came. She was also young and hungry, which, in her agent, suited Trish just fine. "How are you doing? You're finishing up the last of the *Dark Touch* work, aren't you?"

"It's coming along." Trish set down her briefcase and took a seat. "I've got one more scene to finish today and I'm done. I'll get it over to Westhoff's offices tomorrow."

"Great. We should also talk about—"

A trio of people entered the room, cutting Roberta off. Trish took a deep breath. She went through the introductions almost mechanically, all her senses on the alert for Ty to walk in.

But he didn't appear.

Trish flushed when it came to shaking hands with Charlie. She'd only seen him from the back that day at Ty's, so his face was unfamiliar. His smile was surprisingly kind. He held her gaze for a moment. "I've heard a lot of good things about you."

"I hope I'll live up to them," she replied.

He grinned and turned back to the rest of the room. "Okay, people, the gang's all here. Let's figure out how to make ourselves a movie."

Trish shot a look around the room. Ty wasn't there.

At the head of the table, Charlie was handing around production notes and launching into discussion. She had to face the obvious: she wasn't going to see Ty at the meeting.

It was only then that she admitted to herself how much she'd wanted to.

SHE SAT AT HER DESK that afternoon, staring at the screen of her laptop. The scene needed to be finished by morning because Westhoff was planning to shoot it the following night. Focus was important; she had to get this right. Somehow she kept finding herself staring into space, instead.

Okay, so Ty never showed at the meeting. That was good, she reminded herself. He'd told her he'd keep business and whatever was between them personally separate. He was holding to their agreement—so well, in fact, that he was apparently extricating himself from the business end, also.

So why couldn't she feel happy about it? Trish rose and crossed the room to drop down on the sofa. For more than a week, she'd been a bundle of nerves over the idea of seeing Ty—what to wear, what to say, how to act, how to show him that she was getting along just fine without him. His absence should have been a relief.

It had just made her miss him all the more.

She let her head fall back against the pillows and pressed her palms against her eyes. She had to get past it. Clearly, Ty had or he'd have been in the meeting. Of course, that was no surprise with him—out of sight was out of mind. She raised her head, staring at the door. Then she saw it as though it were happening again—the look on his face that night when he'd left, the sound of his voice when he'd told her that he loved her.

And the rusty gate inside her burst fully open and she believed.

Oh God. Trish sucked in a long breath. She'd listened, but she'd never really heard. How could she have been so caught up in herself? How had she been so concerned about protecting herself that she'd managed to totally and completely screw everything up?

She stood and began pacing. How insecure could she have been? He'd told her over and over that he cared, that she was different, that he wanted this. And all she'd done was throw it back at him. If he'd hurt her, she'd hurt him just as much. She'd made him fight and push until he got tired of fighting and pushing. And now he'd just gone away.

She should have been happy that her predictions had come true. Instead, she fell back into her chair and curled up into a ball. The moments stretched out into misery.

She stirred, finally. The script still had to be finished, whether she felt like it or not. Dragging herself back to the desk, she sat in front of her computer. It was just a few lines, just a matter of fixing the final encounter between the hero and the heroine, after he had discovered her deception, after he'd accused her of betrayal.

In the original, it had only taken an apology for everything to be right, but Trish knew that things were never that easy. Her fingers began to type. The hero would strike out, the heroine would close down and protect herself. The hero would freeze her out.

But what happened after?

Trish's fingers slowed, then sped up again. A woman who'd risked her life to catch a murderer and save the man she loved wouldn't just walk away at a few harsh words. When the emotion was really there, it stayed. And a woman in love would come back and she'd keep coming back until she convinced him. *I am not giving up on you, John,* Trish wrote, and then stopped.

Could it really be that simple? Could it be as simple as knowing what she felt and then just telling him? Trusting him enough for them both? She swallowed and thought again of Ty standing at her door. *Looks like I'll have to have enough faith for both of us.* "No," she said out loud. "Not anymore."

And a sudden lightness filled her until it was difficult to breathe.

THE NIGHT SHOOT looked like some sort of military operation. And, like a military operation, she was sure it had lines of security designed to keep fans from mobbing Ty. Trish walked in, crossing her fingers that she'd get on the set. Her passport was the brown envelope in her hands that held Westhoff's missing scene.

It wasn't as though she was going to interrupt Ty when he was shooting. She knew better than that. She'd just wait outside his trailer, maybe get a few minutes alone with him. What was within her couldn't wait until morning.

She slipped past a barricade looking ahead to where a few assistants and extras milled about. She couldn't stop herself from scanning for Ty.

"Stop right there." The security officer moved to intercept her. "This is a restricted area, ma'am."

"I need to get on the set," she told him.

"You'll have to check with him." He pointed to another security guard at the next barrier who held a clipboard full of papers.

Trish nodded; anything that got her closer to Ty would work. "I'm one of the screenwriters," she explained to the second guard. It wasn't a lie, not really.

"Name?"

"Trish Dawson."

He flipped through his sheets, then shook his head. "I don't see it."

"I need to drop off a scene to Dale Westhoff. If you can just let me in I can prove I'm supposed to be here." At least she hoped she could.

The security guard wasn't having it. He crossed his arms and stood foursquare. "Authorized personnel only."

"But I..." She looked beyond him. "Wait, there's someone I know. Jack—" she called out, quick relief washing over her.

It was the assistant director that she'd met in rehearsal. "Jack, hey, remember me? The one who's working on the script?" She held up her envelope.

Recognition dawned. "Oh, oh yeah. Hey, Trish, how ya doing? She's okay," he said to the security guard, who moved aside for her.

"How's the shoot going?"

"Good. We're just finishing up a chase scene. Want to come watch?"

"Sure. Oh, and here are the changes to that last scene."

"Great. I'll get these to Dale." He took the envelope and flagged a passing woman. "Stacy, this is Trish Dawson, who's doing the script rewrites. Can you take her over where she can watch the shoot? Stacy's one of our production assistants. She'll take good care of you," he said in an aside to Trish.

"Thanks," she said gratefully.

Arc lights lit the street, which gleamed wet, even though it hadn't rained in days. "It makes it look better for filming," Stacy explained. The building was brick, the fire escape threading down was rusty. "At the window, look—" she murmured, pointing to the second-story window, a stone's throw away from them.

Trish shivered in her leather bomber jacket, but not from cold.

With a clack of the clapper, the scene burst into action. A figure climbed swiftly down the fire-escape ladder, and ran away. In the same instant, Ty exploded out of the window, leaping off the fire escape to the ground. He was up and running almost before he'd landed—all strength and sinew, catching up with the fugitive in a few yards and tackling him.

"He looks good, doesn't he?" Stacy whispered. "You'd never guess this is the tenth take of this scene."

Trish couldn't answer, mostly because she couldn't get her breath. The two figures rose to their feet and began heading back toward the cameras. Ty's narrow black trousers and jacket looked battered from the long night. His jacket sleeve flapped with a cinematic tear.

"Dale, don't you have enough by now?" The actor playing the fugitive groused as they came near, rubbing his elbow. "I'm getting beat up here."

Trish saw Dale behind the camera now. "Okay, I guess we can all take fifteen," he agreed.

Ty raised his hands over his head and clapped a few times, walking tiredly toward the cameras. His hair was disheveled, and fake blood marred one cheek. His eyes were shadowed, she saw as he neared.

And she saw the instant he recognized her, and watched his weariness drop away.

This wasn't how she'd planned it, Trish thought feverishly, heart thudding. Where were the words she'd rehearsed, the careful explanation, the polished dialog?

Ty met her in three swift steps and then swept her into his arms.

It was the only reality she needed. She didn't notice the murmurs from the crew, didn't care. Ty was the only person who mattered, for always.

"I can't believe you're here," he murmured, just holding her.

Her laugh was half a sob. "Even I figure things out eventually."

He framed her face with his hands. "You mean that? Really?"

Of all her possible answers, she chose the simplest. "Yes."

His kiss held hopes and dreams and tenderness. *He* was her future. How could she not have seen it?

Ty pulled her closer. "I meant what I said. I'm not giving up on you," he murmured. "Ever."

Trish raised her head and kissed him. "You won't have to."

It was all that needed to be said.

* * * * *

You're invited to the next meeting of the
SEX & SUPPER CLUB
coming in December 2004!
Don't miss Cilla's story...
NOTHING BUT THE BEST
Blaze #164.

If you enjoyed what you just read,
then we've got an offer you can't resist!

Take 2 bestselling love stories FREE!
Plus get a FREE surprise gift!

HARLEQUIN®
Temptation®

It's hot...and it's out of control!

**The days might be getting cooler...
but the nights are hotter than ever!**

Don't miss these bold, ultra-sexy books!

#988 HOT & BOTHERED
by KATE HOFFMANN
August 2004

#991 WICKEDLY HOT
by LESLIE KELLY
September 2004

#995 SEDUCE ME
by JILL SHALVIS
October 2004

#999 WE'VE GOT TONIGHT
by JACQUIE D'ALESSANDRO
November 2004

Don't miss this thrilling foursome!

www.eHarlequin.com

HTITF